A ROGUE'S
DECAMERON

ESSENTIAL PROSE SERIES 143

Canada Council
for the Arts

Conseil des Arts
du Canada

ONTARIO ARTS COUNCIL
CONSEIL DES ARTS DE L'ONTARIO

an Ontario government agency
un organisme du gouvernement de l'Ontario

Canadä

Guernica Editions Inc. acknowledges the support of the Canada Council
for the Arts and the Ontario Arts Council. The Ontario Arts Council
is an agency of the Government of Ontario.

We acknowledge the financial support of the Government of Canada.

A ROGUE'S DECAMERON

STAN ROGAL

**GUERNICA
EDITIONS**
TORONTO • BUFFALO • LANCASTER (U.K.)
2018

Copyright © 2018, Stan Rogal and Guernica Editions Inc.
All rights reserved. The use of any part of this publication,
reproduced, transmitted in any form or by any means, electronic,
mechanical, photocopying, recording or otherwise stored
in a retrieval system, without the prior consent
of the publisher is an infringement of the copyright law.

Michael Mirolla, editor
Errol F. Richardson, cover design
David Moratto, interior design
Guernica Editions Inc.
1569 Heritage Way, Oakville, (ON), Canada L6M 2Z7
2250 Military Road, Tonawanda, N.Y. 14150-6000 U.S.A.
www.guernicaeditions.com

Distributors:
University of Toronto Press Distribution,
5201 Dufferin Street, Toronto (ON), Canada M3H 5T8
Gazelle Book Services, White Cross Mills
High Town, Lancaster LA1 4XS U.K.

First edition.
Printed in Canada.

Legal Deposit – Third Quarter
Library of Congress Catalog Card Number: 2017964539
Library and Archives Canada Cataloguing in Publication
Rogal, Stan, 1950-, author
A rogue's Decameron / Stan Rogal. -- First edition.

(Essential prose series ; 143)
Short stories.
Issued in print and electronic formats.
ISBN 978-1-77183-105-5 (softcover).
--ISBN 978-1-77183-106-2 (EPUB).
--ISBN 978-1-77183-107-9 (Kindle)

I. Title. II. Series: Essential prose series ; 143
PS8585.O391R64 2018   C813'.54   C2018-900138-0   C2018-900139-9

*This book is dedicated to Jacquie,
by far the more venturesome—
"What a long, strange trip it's been."*
—GRATEFUL DEAD

CONTENTS

CONTENTS

"*You must read, you must persevere, you must sit up nights, you must inquire, and exert the utmost power of your mind. If one way does not lead to the desired meaning, take another; if obstacles arise, then still another; until, if your strength holds out, you will find that clear which at first looked dark.*"
—GIOVANNI BOCCACCIO

"*I will eviscerate you in fiction. Every pimple, every character flaw. I was naked for a day; you will be naked for eternity.*"
—GEOFFREY CHAUCER IN *A KNIGHT'S TALE*

A ROGUE'S DECAMERON:
PROLOGUE

It was an evening adult course run June/July through George Brown College, eight Thursday night sessions of study and comparison: Boccaccio's *The Decameron* to Chaucer's *The Canterbury Tales*. The course comprised reading and discussion of the two original texts as well as investigating adaptations, whether stories, stage, film or art. What began with twenty eager souls had dwindled to a migratory twelve to fourteen by week seven, out of which six or eight of us might gather afterward at a local pub to knock back a few pints, share plates of fries, nachos and wings and chat about the latest developments. Tonight had been an outing to catch Pasolini's film version of *The Decameron* playing at the indie Royal Theatre in Little Italy, so a very *a propos* setting. The film was hokey, but entertaining enough, and the stalwarts headed to the Café Diplomatico afterward where we had a reservation on the patio and where we could order beer pitchers, wine carafes, pizza slices and immerse ourselves in conversation.

There were seven of us from the class plus two partners who had tagged along for the movie and a third partner who joined us later on the patio for refreshments. This third partner didn't appear too thrilled to be there and pretty much remained glued to his cell when he wasn't otherwise leaned back in his chair rolling his eyes in a bored manner at the sky or else checking out the female action parading the patio and surrounding area of College and Clinton streets, an exercise that didn't go unnoticed by his ... what? Friend? Girlfriend? Wife? Relative? His first appearance among us and I wondered: Why now? The woman—early thirties, Asian, real estate agent by name of Karen—generally tried to ignore his behaviour and I guessed she'd only invited him as a polite gesture and was maybe surprised he'd actually shown. She'd introduced him as Mark. That was it, nothing more: "Hey everyone, meet Mark."

Hi Mark, et cetera, from the gang.

Karen liked her red wine, but it didn't like her and— as a rule—by about glass number three, she'd be shit-faced, laughing for no particular reason, talking loudly and leaning on anyone in close vicinity. Perhaps it was because she only weighed about ninety-eight pounds soaking wet, or maybe it was simple DNA. Whatever, she could either be a whole lot of fun or else a whole lot of headache. At this point it was too early to tell, though I was betting on the latter, given her friend. Mark ordered a double bar scotch straight up, gave it a taste, twisted his lips and complained about the quality—or lack thereof —just loud enough for all and sundry to hear. Karen tore the glass from his hand, banged back the contents herself and told him not to be such a cheap bastard next time and order a better brand. He could afford it.

"Maybe I'll do that," he said, and sloppily poured some beer from a nearby pitcher into the whiskey glass.

He struck me immediately as a first-rate asshole.

I knew as much—or as little—about the others at the table. Our conversation generally centred around the course content and maybe got a tad more personal as we became more lubricated, though, by that time, who remembered much beyond name, job and the odd detail such as dog or cat owner, vegetarian or omnivore, kids or no?

If push came to shove, I knew that Paula and Gail were a lesbian couple in their fifties, Gail working as an Arts Administrator with the Toronto Arts Council and Paula a social worker specializing in street youth. They took classes together as a night out. Gail drank red wine and Paula enjoyed the local craft brews, organic whenever possible. They were both vegetarian.

Monica was in her early forties, worked in retail selling appliances at the Bay. Her partner, Aaron, was in construction, didn't belong to the class but showed up most nights for drinks, his preference being bottled Molson Canadian. Nice guy and the two seemed to get along well.

Another couple was Anthony and Portia, early sixties, the only ones here with honest-to-goodness Italian backgrounds and who visited the heritage country with regularity to spend time with friends and family. Both retired public school teachers. Thank God for that, Anthony would cross himself. The way things are today—the violence, the sex, the drugs ... He'd pause here and toss us all a look. And that's just the parents! He'd belly laugh and slap his thighs and Portia right along with him. We'd all heard this line, of course, like, a million times before. Anyway, Anthony took the class and Portia would always be waiting for the group at the assigned rendezvous spot, sipping a gin and tonic through a straw before switching to a glass of white wine. She was always eager to hear the complete details of the lecture and the surrounding discussion. Anthony was happy to oblige—along with embellishments—as he shared in the beer pitcher with Paula.

Naomi was early fifties, fancied herself an actress, though appeared to earn most of her income teaching French immersion and ESL. Always seemed to be taking a different acting class or voice class or movement class with the latest brilliant instructor, until it was time to find a different class with the next latest brilliant instructor. She somehow let us know early on she did not want to be referred to as Afro-American as she was born in Scarborough and had never even visited the "dark continent," as she called it. Also a red wine drinker.

That left me, and the less said the better, except to say, red wine was also my beverage of choice.

The evening progressed with the usual banter to do with the course and much time spent going over scenes from the film and laughing, mainly, at the absurdities of the time and how things have changed, specifically in terms of the Church, which had been a mainstay of humorous attacks by writers, the subject now grown far too serious given the court cases concerning sexual misconduct, whether improprieties within the flock at large, or worse, abuse of the children. Also, even, the manner in which the characters of the film so easily fell into bed with one another and no thought of either the moral or ethical implications nor the consequences of such rash behaviour, nor the need to wear protection.

"Yeah," Anthony said smiling, "all good fun until someone loses an eye."

"Willing suspension of disbelief," Portia said. "That's why we go to movies."

"Oh, I don't know. Sounds just like the sixties to me," Aaron said laughing.

"Sounds like the nineties to me," Monica said.

"Uh-huh?" Aaron leaned in to her. "And what were you doing in the nineties that you didn't tell me about?"

"Wouldn't you like to know," she said, purring, and we all laughed.

"Face it," Gail said. "Same shit, different day. Nothing really changes. As a race, we're still driven by our appetites."

"I'll drink to that," Karen said.

"Speaking of which," Naomi said. "Isn't it odd how our attractive young professor hasn't made it out for a drink with us since the first couple of weeks? He always has to hurry away and, I wonder—does he, in fact, use the night as an excuse to hook up with someone for a bit of hanky-panky on the side, the gold band on his wedding finger notwithstanding?" We all gave it some serious consideration. "I mean, don't you remember that sort of attractive bleached blonde among us at the start with the duck lips and silicone tits, also flashing a large rock on her wedding finger and who was always cornering him with questions, and who suddenly disappeared? What happened there, do you think? After all, how often

5

can you teach a course that has infidelity as a major theme and not want to experiment with the notion?"

An intriguing speculation, I thought. We all nodded and, I'm sure, did our own quick mental check of the group and, while the idea appeared somewhat amusing, I don't believe anyone was prepared and/or motivated to make the leap. I could be wrong. In fact, Karen was a real cutie, though too young for me — beyond blaming the booze — and Naomi had a rather evil sense of humour, which I found attractive. Still, not attractive enough to pursue, especially as she'd given me no provocation or hint to suggest otherwise.

"You don't really think …? Do you? The two of them?" Karen was still back trying to puzzle out the professor and the blonde. I didn't know if it was the two of them *per se* she couldn't envision together between the sheets, or the concept of an affair in general. People took sidelong looks at each other, nodded, grinned and so on. We all raised our glasses and drank, pondering.

It was getting late and the inevitable subject of "too bad the course was coming to an end" and someone — I think it was Portia — wondered if there wasn't some way to keep the group together a bit longer as it was always fun to meet up and share stories. Naturally, we were all fairly warm and fuzzy with the alcohol by this point and already feeling vaguely nostalgic, so we all agreed. Slightly earlier in the evening, slightly more sober, perhaps a couple of us might have pointed out what a truly wrongheaded idea this was and why it could never work — why it DOES never work — and history has proven time and time again that it's always best to allow things to live out their natural span, then let it go.

As I said, we were not of our right minds and, in fact, it was me who proposed an idea. What if, I offered, we set up a situation akin to that of the characters in the books we've been studying?

All eyes focused on me and everyone was attentive. No one spoke but the looks on their faces said: Tell us more. I continued. As it stands, there are ten of us gathered, a mix of male and female, same as in the books. What if we decided to each write a story based on the major themes of *The Decameron* and/or *The Canterbury Tales*? Meaning: lust, cunning, deceit, revenge, jealousy, love, sex, deception, adultery, religion, bawdy humour, literary allusions and so on and so forth. Meaning: pretty much the same major themes of any time or place. We make Toronto the central setting, though characters can come and go from the city to engage in whatever adventure, from the normal everyday to the odd to the fantastic—such is the nature of the tale. Next week is the final class, so we can plan to meet back here at the Dip in two weeks with our completed stories. We make the stories anonymous, read them aloud to each other and try to figure out who wrote which story. Then we repeat the process every two weeks until we run out of steam. Or stories.

"Mark knows SFA about Boccaccio or Chaucer," Karen said. "He thought the Pasolini film was a gangster movie." She leaned back and laughed hysterically.

"We can ask someone else from the class," I said. "Shouldn't be a problem."

"You think I can't write a story?" I wasn't sure if Mark directed this at Karen or at the table in general.

"I know you can't," Karen said. "All you can do is fucking text." She mimed him pounding the keypad.

"That's okay, we can get someone."

"No way," Mark said. "I'm in. What's the big deal? I know a thing or two about jealousy and deceit, don't I, Karen?"

That comment made our ears prick. We looked to Karen for her response.

Karen made a rude sound with her lips. "You think you do. But then, you think you know everything."

"It's not a problem," I said, wanting to keep the peace. "We'll ask someone else."

"I said I'm in! I'll write a fucking story. You think I can't? Piece o'cake."

Karen mimicked Mark: "*I'll write a fucking story.* Right. He'll pay his secretary to write it for him."

"Don't worry, I'll write it, alright. Watch me."

Everyone was uncomfortable and things got pretty quiet for a moment. Paula jumped in.

"Great then! Mark's okay to contribute a story. You heard him. What about Aaron and Portia? Are you guys okay?" The two nodded. "Everyone else?" There was mumbled approval. "Terrific!" She turned to me. "How do we make it anonymous?"

I pulled a deck of cards from my shoulder bag, separated the spades, eliminated the face cards, shuffled the remainder and dealt them out face down.

"Here we are," I said. "The cards run one to ten. When

you finish your story, tuck the card under the paper clip. In two weeks we all write our card and our name on a slip of paper and put them on the table. At the end, we turn them over to see which person belongs to which story." I gave them all my email so they could get hold of me if there were any questions or problems.

Around eleven we finished our drinks, finished our goodbyes and everyone sailed out into the night.

Next morning I sat with a coffee over the computer and was met with my first response. I checked the time it was sent: 12:32 a.m. It was from Karen and stated very simply and succinctly: Mark and I are out. I sent his dumb ass packing so it's over. I likely won't be at class next week either. Sorry.

Anthony and Portia emailed a few days later, claimed there were family matters they had to attend to and were flying off to Italy ASAP so would also miss the final session. By Wednesday Gail and Paula had pulled out due to "unforeseen circumstances" and Naomi sent a note saying she'd scored a commercial being shot in Montreal, so *au revoir* and *bonne chance*!

When I arrived at the class Thursday, Monica and Aaron admitted that maybe they'd been a tad overconfi-dent at the café—or maybe a tad drunk—and soon came to realize they had neither the ambition nor the skill set to write a story. They handed me their cards. Aaron joked they wanted to be sure I was playing with a full deck. Perhaps the others felt the same because the professor met me with several envelopes either dropped off or mailed in to the college, which I assumed contained the rest of the missing cards. I stuck them in my shoulder bag and sat through the slimmed-down class wondering if the excuses were all real or if the notion of writing a story had actually filled everyone with so much dread that most dared not even show their faces. To be completely honest, I was also feeling a sense of relief as I was having great difficulty coming up with even a single story idea that might warrant serious pursuit and figured it was probably for the best that the others had bowed out.

Afterward, several of us headed to the bar. We were joined by the professor this time. The blonde woman with the duck lips and silicone tits also joined us, apologizing for her long absence, saying it was due to her father having had a heart attack and her needing to fly to Florida to help take care of him as the wife/mother had left him years ago to take up with a plastic surgeon in California. Her father doing better, she returned to Toronto and wanted to show up at the bar to say goodbye to everyone.

The professor offered his condolences and said that he too was dealing with family issues—his wife had fractured her ankle while walking the dog and he had to be around to take care of her for several weeks. She was also much improved.

I wondered what was more improbable, the stories these two just told of their whereabouts or the one Naomi had presented earlier? At any rate, as per her prior behaviour in class, and as if this sharing of family hardship provided a further bond between them, the blonde woman concentrated her attentions wholly on the professor and he responded in kind, the two of them remaining lost in their own little world, more or less oblivious to the other members of the class. So, as they billed and cooed, the rest of us engaged in small talk, sipped our drinks and eventually parted company. By the time I slipped away, the blonde woman and the professor sat so close together, you couldn't fit a cigarette paper between their thighs.

Like they say, the road to hell is paved with good intentions, I reminded myself. A shame, really, everyone seemed so eager. Ah, well, that's the way it goes, I guess. It was obviously a done deal, everyone separated to parts unknown, and, if the stories were ever to be actually written, it appeared they'd have to write themselves. Unless ...? I was suddenly struck by a rather strange notion, as: *What if?* I fished the deck of cards out of my shoulder bag and tapped the package edge against my palm.

What if and why not? I asked myself.

Why not, indeed.

THE BUTCHER WIFE'S TALE

*In which—upon her husband arriving early into
the shop—Rosa conceals her lover in the meat
locker then proceeds to devise a story in
which she is able to continue her tryst while
getting her husband to grant her every request.*

Rosa arched her broad back against the cushioned arm
of the couch. She stretched her plump left leg across
the worn leather and ground her French heeled shoe into
the pine floorboards. Her equally plump right leg hung
quivering in the air, a slight pair of damp pink lace panties dangling from a surprisingly delicate ankle. Her dress
was unbuttoned at the neck and a pair of exquisitely large
breasts danced half-in, half-out of an industrial wired
bra. Two clumsy hands—not her own—grappled with the
breasts, rolled the flesh and pinched the nipples. The
hands were attached to two thin arms that threaded down
Rosa's round belly and disappeared beneath her skirts.
Her own hands were kneading what could only be a head
hard at work between her thighs. Rosa jutted her chin
and bit her lower lip. Scattered among jagged breaths and
sobs, small joyous squeals emanated from her flushed
throat.

"Yes, yes," she softly moaned. "Yes."

Sounds of creaking stairs snapped the pair's dalliance still as a polaroid.

"My husband," she hissed, and with a quick shove of foot to shoulder ungently separated a mouth from her more private parts. The young man attached to that same mouth performed an awkward back somersault. There was a combination abject fear and outright panic written on his face. Rosa slipped her panties into place, tucked the girls into their Lycra harness and hastily buttoned up. She grabbed the youth by an elbow, dragged him toward the meat locker, yanked open the door and flung him roughly inside. She placed an index finger to her lips: *Ssh!* She eased the door shut, tip-toed across the floor, positioned herself on a corner of an oak desk and proceeded to flip though a tattered issue of *Canadian Living Magazine.* The young man, meanwhile, scraped a spot through the ice on the small window and eyeballed the scene. Rosa motioned with a hand: *Down!*

"Carlito, my sweet? You're up early." She gave her raven hair a flip.

"Mm," he said grunting. "Couldn't sleep."

"Oh? Anything wrong, love?"

"Nothing new. Work to do. Bills to pay."

"Ah, my poor little man. Always worried. Come to Rosa." She extended her neck and twisted her cheek. Carlito leaned in for a peck.

"You're hot," Carlito said, stroking her cheek with his own. "Cold as hell down here and you're hot." He clapped his hands together and smiled. "My little furnace." He surveyed the room and spotted a denim jacket crumpled on the couch. Rosa followed his eyes. "What were you up to all by yourself?"

"Did I say I was all by myself?" Rosa saw Carlito flex his ham hock hands into fists. He was a large man and still muscular, despite the extra pounds age had added to his waist. Rosa was several years younger and no lightweight herself, though she resembled a mere slip-of-a-thing in comparison. She took a deep breath, puffed out her ample chest and cocked her head coquettishly. "In fact, I'm not all by myself, I'm entertaining a customer."

"Uh-huh? Where?"

"There." Rosa indicated the freezer. "He's checking out the meat."

"Before business hours?"

"He heard you offered the best meat in Bloorcourt Village. In his excitement, he got the hours wrong. I caught him peering through the shop window. What could I do? I invited him in. Couldn't let him catch his death. Middle of winter and all. I don't think he's any too bright. That thin jacket of his wouldn't keep a cat warm. Anyway, he said he wanted a side of our finest pork. A side! He said money was no object."

"What did you tell him?"

"What do you think? I bumped it a dollar a pound and he didn't even blink. *Anything*, he said. *For a taste. A sniff.*"

"Good girl."

"I told him to choose whatever slab appealed most to him. He's been in there some time now. He's young and I don't think he knows much about meat, really, except for eating. The various cuts and so on. The tender parts. The juicy bits. Like I said, a tad dim. Enthusiastic, though, and a healthy appetite, I imagine." Rosa swung her legs off the desk, dashed to the freezer, ripped open the door. "How's it going in there? Find something you like? Daniel, isn't it?"

"Yes," he said, shivering from the locker and rubbing his shoulders. "It's difficult to choose. It all looks so good." A faint white rime coated his cheeks and chin.

"This is my husband, Carlito."

The men nodded each to each.

"Yes, it's a challenge, isn't it? Hanging there, they all look the same, yet each one is different. Carlito's the expert, aren't you sweet? Why don't you go in and give us a demonstration?"

"What? Oh, sure, I'll just grab my coat."

"Oh, don't be such a baby. Get in there. How long can it take?" She wrapped an arm around his waist, popped him into the fog and shut the door except for a crack big enough to stick her nose. "We'll watch from this side. Make sure to speak up so we can hear." Rosa bent at the waist and Daniel perched over top of her. "Go on!"

Carlito shrugged and shuffled into the freezer. He grabbed a black handle and pressed a button. A motor hummed and sides of pork appeared in a row attached by hooks to a chain link assembly line. He released the button and presented the first carcass. He pointed out the different cuts. His lips moved but he was too far away to be heard.

"What? Louder!" Rosa yelled. "We can't hear you.

Louder!" She raised her skirts, used her thumbs to wriggle her panties down her legs onto the floor and stepped a foot free. She reached up to Daniel's waist, freed his belt, unbuttoned and unzipped his jeans. He was still wearing his condom. *Ah, youth*, she thought. She gripped his erection and directed the tip into the correct hole, all the while keeping close watch on her husband through the gap. Her actions were aided considerably by the fact that Daniel wore no underwear, though she proved otherwise dexterous for a woman equipped with hands that looked like they could crack walnuts.

"Oh, oh, ah," she squealed, as Daniel drove in deeper.

"What?" Carlito shouted. "This one?" He cradled the second side of pork in his arms and offered a view of the empty cavity framed in spareribs. Rosa opened the door wide enough to get a meaty arm through and waved at him.

"No, no, not that one. A different one." Rosa felt another thrust. "Oh! Try a different one."

Carlito twisted his face and shook his head. "For chrissakes, Rosa—they're all the same," he whispered. "There is no different one."

"No, I told the boy, something special. He's paying for it after all. Top dollar."

Daniel straightened and stuck his face in the window. He squinted and could barely make out Carlito due to the dim light and accumulation of ice and haze. He flashed a wide smile in the man's general direction and rode Rosa harder, even as the sides of pork made their appointed rounds. Rosa's breathing sped up, her voice got jerkier, she reached behind with both hands, grabbed Daniel's ass and returned his fervour, thrust for urgent thrust.

"Yes!" she cried. "Yes! Yes! Oh, yes!"

"Yes?" Carlito replied. "Yes? You're sure? 'Cause once I bring this bastard out, I'm not coming back in, clear?"

"Yes. Clear. That's it. That's it. That's the one. That's it. Ah! Yes!"

"Finally," Carlito said, unhooking the chosen side and slinging it over a shoulder.

Daniel withdrew from Rosa, peeled off the condom, knotted it, scrambled into his pants and collapsed on the couch. He held the condom up between two fingers, unsure as where to deposit it. Rosa snatched the thing, rolled it inside a Kleenex, tucked the wad down her bra and once again shimmied into her panties and smoothed her skirts.

Carlito stomped from the freezer, breezed past the makeshift office area to the other side of the room and tossed the carcass onto the butcher block.

"OK, there it is. How's our boy want to pay for it?"

"We already discussed that. Layaway plan."

"That's become real popular lately. You sure he'll come through?"

"He better, otherwise I'll take it out of his hide." Rosa shook a fist at the boy and growled.

Carlito laughed and wagged a finger. "And she ain't foolin', so watch yourself. She's got a whole list just like you. You don't wanna be on the wrong side of this one, no way." He and Rosa winked and nodded like they shared a joke.

"I understand, sir, and I swear I won't flinch in my obligations."

"Uh-huh. Good to hear. How's he getting it home?"

"I said you'd deliver it personal."

"Oh yeah? My brother borrowed the van for the day, remember?"

"He's right around the corner on Salem. Easy-peasy."

"There's a snow storm raging out there."

"Oh, for crying out loud, what a big baby you are. Afraid of a little snow."

"C'mon Rosa." Carlito saw Rosa was determined. "I guess ... if he gives me a hand, should be OK."

"Are you crazy? Look at him—he weighs maybe one hundred forty pounds soaking wet. Besides, he's got a bad back, don't you, honey? Hurt it pumping."

"Pumping?"

"He works at his dad's gas station. Pumps gas. Isn't that right?"

The boy shook his head in agreement.

"The low foreign jobs, especially. All that bending." Rosa bent and wiggled her ass. "It's killer."

"You seem to know a lot about this boy. Are you sure you just met?"

"I said his mind was a bit slow. There's nothing wrong with his tongue. Started flapping as soon as he walked in." She formed her fingers into a pair of moving lips. "Goes a mile a minute. Talk, talk, talk."

"You mean he managed to get a word in edgewise?"

"Shut up. Anyway, he's the customer and there's no need for him to be delivering his own meat when there's a big strong man like you around."

"Uh-huh. How old are you, boy?"

"Nineteen."

"Nineteen, eh? Some advice—never marry for love the way I did, it'll kill ya. Look at me, fifty going on eighty 'cause I can't say no. Meanwhile she's thirty-eight going on eighteen."

"Don't fill his head with nonsense."

"OK, OK. You win. Again. I'm going." Carlito tossed on a coat, hat, gloves and boots. He wrapped the carcass in butcher paper, secured it with heavy string and draped the package around his neck.

"Here." Rosa stuffed a slip of paper into his pocket. "I've written the address so you don't get lost. Speak directly to Daniel's mother. She'll make you a nice hot *um garoto*. Right?"

"Right," Daniel said. "I'll text her you're coming." He punched the phone pad.

"And take your time. I need to go over the finer details of the layaway plan so there are no misunderstandings."

"That's good. Don't want you to take on more than you can handle."

"Don't worry about me. You know when I have a job to do I put my back into it."

"Fine. I go, I go." Carlito turned the door handle and ducked into the storm. A few snowflakes whistled in, spun madly, finally settled and melted on the floor.

Rosa pursed her lips, rolled her eyes and sat next to Daniel. She squeezed his knee and slowly crawled her fingers up his leg to his crotch.

"And how's my little man doing, hmm? Still hungry?"

Daniel smiled goofily. The two began to laugh. They laughed and laughed.

THE DETECTIVE'S TALE

In which a detective's search for truth leads him to peek behind the veil of apparent religious beliefs and supernatural occurrences.

"In the Greater Toronto area, provincial police say there have been nearly forty wheel-offs in the past twelve and a half months. In that period, there were forty-three incidents of flying wheels, twenty-seven of them hitting vehicles and injuring nineteen people."

— *The Toronto Star*

The trucker relates his story to a young police officer who listens politely, nods and jots down whatever shorthand version he's gathered into an official looking notepad. The trucker is quite animated and gesticulates wildly with his hands and head. He tugs at the brim of his baseball cap, drags his fingers through the stubble of one cheek and pulls at his chin. He throws his arms in the air and points in this and that direction. Meanwhile, the normal flow of traffic zips up and down Black Creek Road, slowed only by the odd rubbernecker trying to catch a glimpse of *what the hell's up?* Otherwise, folks with things to do, places to go, people to meet. Also, nowhere convenient to pull over, park, take a short stroll and investigate the action.

Palm heels press into horns: C'mon, move it buddy!

"It never should've happened. I don't believe it. I been drivin' rigs over twenty years and nothin' like this has ever happened to me before. I mean, never."

"Uh-huh." The young officer answers nonplussed, as if he's heard it all a thousand times before. And perhaps he has, especially recently.

"It's God's truth, I swear. The truck was inspected top to bottom just three days ago. I check it again myself every time before I set out. I don't take it on the road unless I've tightened every wheel nut by hand. There's no way. No way in the world." The trucker paces a small section of grassy shoulder. He continues to emphasize his words by stabbing the air with his hands and head. He whips off his cap and slaps it against a corner of the front fender. "God damn," he says. The truck itself remains resolute, tipped slightly to one side on the sloped embankment.

The officer taps his notepad with the tip of a mechanical pencil. "Maybe not," he says. "But there it is." He flips the notepad shut and wraps his eyes behind a pair of Foster Grants. The trucker wipes his brow with a blue and white checked handkerchief and replaces the cap on his head. The two men squint across the four lanes of heated asphalt to where a crowd of pedestrians, leashed dogs and cyclists has formed a tight circle around a clutch of other police officers. The officers attempt to control the situation as best they can, calling out orders and waving nightsticks in the air. They are firm in their words and behaviours, without being overtly threatening.

All in a day's work.

"Move on now. Nothing to see here. Move on," the officers repeat as they attempt to cordon the area off with yellow tape. Onlookers try to see beyond the barrier of uniformed bodies; some raise digital cameras or cell phones above their heads hoping to get a shot of what lies at the centre. Dogs tug at collars and crawl between and around legs. A flock of starlings pulses the clear blue sky.

"No pictures. Move on please. Let the police do their job. Move along now. Go on about your business. Nothing to see here."

The crowd doesn't move along so much as adjust its position around the periphery. They talk amongst themselves, exchanging shared stories gleaned from the various media and postulating their own ideas and theories around what may or may not be occurring, both here and now specifically, as well as in general.

"It's not natural," one bystander says. "It's gone way beyond that. It's something else entirely."

"Sure it's something else, but what?" another says. "I mean, it's not like a plague of locusts or black flies or a mess of goddamn frogs falling from the skies now, is it?"

"Not yet it ain't," a third says. "Just wait. There's more to this, you'll see."

"Yeah, nothin' good'll come of this, fer sure. No way."

Several other folks pitch in as one voice, all making tangible a similar mood of fear and foreboding.

"Tip of the iceberg. Calm before the storm. Early warning sign. Before the shit hits the fan. Before all hell breaks loose."

By the pricking of my thumbs, something wicked this way comes.

Everyone with an opinion.

A female officer turns to a second. "What do you make of it?" She glances out the corner of one eye toward the object that is the apparent cause of all the excitement.

"Beats me. Doesn't look like much, sitting there like that."

"No, it doesn't. Do you think anyone from that group will be along?"

"Wouldn't surprise me. They always seem to find out. Usually before we do."

"Yeah, weird."

"Yeah."

"At least it didn't hit anything or kill anyone."

"No."

"At least not this time."

"Yeah, right."

They both nod and return to the task of crowd control.

"Move along, please. Nothing to see here. Move along."

⌒

At police headquarters, detectives Maxwell and Shorter study a wall map indicating a section of highway framed in heavy black felt pen. Maxwell sticks a pin near the intersection of Eglinton Avenue and Black Creek Drive. The pin has a round, red head. Maxwell steps back.

"That's the furthest south so far," Shorter says.

"Yeah. Probably why we were able to get to it before someone else beat us to the punch." Maxwell scratches his shoulder. "They send it off to the lab?"

Shorter rolls her eyes and chuckles. "Sure. But, what do they expect to find? It's a big rubber tire around a metal rim. Same as the rest."

"Yeah." Maxwell remains studying the map, maybe half-expecting the pieces of the puzzle to fall together with the addition of the latest pin. "I know. But I'll tell you what, somebody better find out something and quick. The brass is getting itchy. This is the fifty-seventh wheel-off in less than a year."

"*Reported*," Shorter says.

"Right, right. Reported. And every one of the bastards along the 401 between the Allen Express and the 400. It's like a Devil's Triangle of flying wheels."

"Don't say that too loud." Shorter grins impishly.

"Say what?"

"Devil's Triangle. The press would have a field day and the phones wouldn't stop ringing."

"Yeah. As it is, that stretch of freeway's become a sort of Mecca for every religious fanatico and New Age nutball in the country."

"And points beyond. I hear they've set up charter flights from as far away as Australia. It's become something of a phenomenon."

"Spare me the gruesome details, please. It's bad enough these lunatics are lining the road hoping for a personal glimpse of the miracle." He spits the word 'miracle.' "But, they're interfering with our investigation by stealing the wheels out from under us." Maxwell purses his lips and makes a clucking sound with his tongue. "What do you suppose they do with them, anyway? Sure as hell don't use 'em as swings in the backyard."

"Set them up as shrines, I imagine."

"What, like in their basements? Most of those suckers wouldn't even fit through a normal sized door. You think they take a chainsaw to the wall?"

Shorter throws her hands into the air, like: Maybe, who knows?

At this moment, Gerry Taylor, a reporter for the *Star*, rushes into the office. He always rushes into the office, even if it's simply to say hello. He's about five foot eight, stocky build, nimble, full of energy, type who loves to hear himself talk. Dresses impeccably in the morning— ironed bright white shirt, burgundy silk tie, polished black shoes, sweet breath, clean armpits—and by coffee break he's in sweaty disarray: shirt untucked, stained and wrinkled, tie loose, shoes scuffed, searching for a bathroom in order to gargle and spray.

Otherwise personable and friendly, depending on your inclinations.

"Hey, guys! What's the scoop?" This is Gerry's classic reporter line.

"Don't you ever knock?" Maxwell sits his lanky frame in a chair and clasps his hands behind his neck. He's about thirty-eight years old and going prematurely bald.

Grass doesn't grow on a busy street, he says.

"Waste of time. Sarah, you look lovely. Max, you're as charming as ever."

Outside their jobs, the three are casual friends, get together for a drink or a bite after work, maybe take in the odd movie. At one time, years ago, there was even a romantic rivalry between Gerry and Max over Sarah. Though perhaps this rivalry only existed in the minds of the two men since Sarah never made overtures one way or another. At any rate, it was over now. After Gerry's initial attempts were met with a cool (though civil) reception, he threw in the towel, leaving the way open, he figured, to Max. Then, nothing much materialized between these two either. A few dates, that was it, otherwise a complete washout in terms of establishing any kind of intimate and/or permanent personal relationship.

Gerry never asked why; didn't see the point. After all, it was still the three of them together as friends. That was the main thing, so probably better for all involved in the end. Especially since they often need to work together and who needs the added drama of sexual politics getting in the mix? Besides which, Max is the quiet sort and likely wouldn't have told Gerry even he did ask.

Curious though just the same.

"Any news on the latest miraculous event?"

"Put a sock in it, Gerry."

"What? No believers in the house?" He turns from Max to Sarah. "Sarah? I'm ashamed. Good Catholic girl like you? Your mothers should've raised you better."

"Lapsed Catholic, I'm afraid."

"No such thing. Once in the fold always in the fold. It's like walking around with a bell around your neck. Just takes the slightest breeze to ring it and, *ding*, you're back on your knees reciting one hail Mary, two hail Marys ...”

“Uh-huh, I see.” Sarah fiddles with the gold cross dangled from her necklace. “Well, there’s nothing to report. The wheel’s been hauled off to the lab.” She leans her butt against the edge of the desk and crosses her arms. She has short thick legs, wide hips, a slim waist, long torso and small breasts. She always wears her skirts a few inches below her knees and her blouses buttoned to the top. Her face is roundish with brilliant sad green eyes, chunky chopped red hair, little makeup and pensive full lips. In fact, her lips are her finest feature in that they physically reflect every thought and emotion that runs through her. As now, when they pucker impishly toward Gerry, recognizing that beyond or behind his playful questioning, he is methodically inspecting her body. The former fire that burned inside him may have been reduced to a mere spark over time but it wasn’t out completely and it certainly didn’t prevent him from enjoying some small amount of sexual innuendo and harmless teasing.

Or so he figures. Sarah lifts one foot in front of the other and locks her ankles.

Gerry tosses a look straight back at her. Max catches it all and sighs: Whatever. Gerry being Gerry and par for the course. Some people never learn.

“What about the driver’s story?” Gerry closes in on Sarah. “He claims that the truck had been fully inspected and passed with flying colours.”

“They all claim that,” Sarah says.

"I checked. It was, and it did." Gerry's face leans into Sarah's.

"Then you know as much as we do." Max rises from his chair and grabs his coat. "Let's go out and get a sandwich."

Gerry lets out a laugh, pulls away from Sarah and charges over to the map. "But even you have to admit, it's all beginning to look more than a little strange."

"How so?" Sarah asks.

Sarah and Max enjoyed listening to Gerry repeat the obvious. He had a talent for it. It occurred each time he came in to discuss a story and Sarah wondered whether Gerry was aware of this habit or not. Max had his own theory: Like most reporters, Gerry was a detective wannabe and always considered himself one step ahead.

"Get serious—no flying wheels anywhere else in the country and we've got close to sixty in the past year?" Gerry covers the floor.

"There've been reports ..." Sarah says, raising her eyebrows.

"Unsubstantiated. What about that group that claims responsibility?"

"The Legion of the Almighty? You think they're snapping metal bolts using the power of their minds?" Max says, laughing.

"They say this is an omen from God; a warning that He is about to destroy Toronto the wicked, with them leading the charge."

"Like Sodom and Gomorrah, yeah?" Max asks.

"Precisely."

"To be fair," Sarah says. "There are other groups that claim it's a sign of fundamental change; a rebirth, if you will, and that we're actually entering a stage of renewed hope, freedom and eternal joy; ecstatic love." Her words and tone cause the men's jaws to drop. They are truly dumbfounded and amazed. They stare at her then at each other.

"What?" Max says, as if escaping from a dream. "You mean, like, wheels escaping their bonds, freeing themselves from the tyranny of a cruel, corrupt, corporate and mech-anistic society or something?" He uses his fingers as if to put the words in quotes. "C'mon. Give me a break, please."

"Sarah, the eternal optimist," Gerry says. "Well done. Bravo!"

The men laugh. Sarah sighs and turns her gaze in the direction of the map.

"You hear what they're up to now?" Gerry revs up once again.

"Who?" Max asks.

"The Legion of the Almighty, who've we been talkin' about? They've set up a twenty-four hour candlelight vigil around the grave of that guy who was killed."

There has been one fatality to date. A man in his early thirties, returning home from working the late shift. He and his van were met head-on by a flying wheel. Po-lice pronounced him DOA. Around his neck he wore a St. Christopher medallion.

"Yeah, I heard. I mean, what's that all about?" There's irritation in Max's voice, though perhaps tinged with a hint of lurid intrigue at the same time.

"They figure his body will be resurrected, flaming sword in hand, prepared to slay the infidels. The Second Coming. Fire and blood." Gerry makes a mock, broad swipe with his arm, past Sarah's neck. She twists her lips and glares.

"Great. That's just great." The phone rings and Max answers. "Right. Thanks," he says, and hangs up. "That's what I was afraid of."

"What's up?" Sarah asks.

"The Legion of the Almighty have lain claim to their martyr, now apparently everyone else wants theirs."

"What is it?" Gerry pulls out a pad and pencil.

"There was another wheel-off on the 401 near the Allen Express. When they saw it happening, about a half-dozen people from various factions suddenly broke from the crowd and tried to step into the wheel's path."

"Anyone hurt?" Sarah asks.

"Not by the wheel. A driver coming from the other direction had to swerve to miss the crazed on-rushers. She ran off the side of the road and suffered minor bruises and a few broken ribs."

"It's always the innocent bystander," Gerry says.

"What are we supposed to do? We can't clear them all away. There must be a few thousand of them scattered along the highway and the numbers are growing every day."

⌒

Sarah is correct on this score. Within hours of the media announcing the latest development, thousands more make the pilgrimage to Toronto, with many camping out on both sides of the 401, some in lean-tos and tents, others in vans and motor homes. As they settle in, they begin to pray in their own way and toward their own ends. Most are merely passive onlookers, but several hope to be one of the chosen to be martyred beneath the treads of a flying wheel. Still others arrive to combine the spiritual with the monetary, setting up food and concession stands. Racks of cheap, fake souvenirs and tawdry T-shirts are available. Fortune tellers are plying their trade. Crafts people are out in full force, peddling everything from holy rocks to God's Eyes to matchstick constructions of Mack trucks with missing wheels to glow-in-the-dark wheel nut rosaries.

No one has the faintest idea what might occur, if anything, but each wants to be there when it does. The police are powerless. It's impossible to remove what has become a small city cloistered along the shores of an asphalt river. Threats are of no consequence. Tickets given for breaking various bylaws are immediately tossed on a pile of similar papers or crushed and thrown into makeshift fires. No one gives a good flying fuck about the law. The law is passé; it's obsolete; it's gone bust. Whether awaiting a tragic end or a brighter beginning, the devoted are convinced that the time is near and earthly rules and regulations no longer hold dominion over them.

A plan proposed to ban traffic along the infamous stretch of highway is vetoed by members of City Council. They claim that, not only is it necessary to maintain the free flow of the artery in terms of the greater public good but business, otherwise, is booming due to the flying wheel phenomenon. The city is making money—a shitload of money. While the camped pilgrims themselves are required to purchase basic necessities, the entire city and surrounding area is packed with transient tourists eager to witness the goings on from a safe distance. Hotels and bus lines are even providing day trips, boxed lunches and other refreshments included. One way or another, everyone wants their share of the action; everyone demands their little piece of heaven.

⌒

"Has everyone gone crazy?" Max asks. "Or is it just me?" He paces the office.

"I don't know," Sarah says. "Maybe there's more to it."

"Not you now, too?"

"Remember the guy who was killed?"

"Yeah, yeah, sure. We tried to get his parents to press charges against the trucking company, right? They declined. Instead, they teamed up with the Legion of the Almighty and joined the vigil. Also a rumour some Hollywood agent offered them a cool million for their story if the son comes back to life, which doesn't surprise me these days. Sick."

"His name was James Corrigan. Initials J.C., right? He worked for a place that made kitchen cabinets, making him a sort of carpenter. Get it?"

"What?" Max shoots her a look. "Oh. Oh! OK, OK! Yeah, I get it, I get it, already! I mean, are you kidding me, or what? Huh? You're kidding me, right? C'mon Sarah, get real."

"I'm just saying ..."

"I know what you're saying. I know. Now, you get this—James Corrigan is dead. His head went through a fucking car windshield and he ain't coming back. No way, no how. Furthermore, the next time a wheel comes loose, there'll be a few more martyrs added to the list. Do you want that?" Max stares at Sarah, who doesn't answer. There's a look on her face that Max is familiar with and it scares him. "Sarah? Sarah?"

"I don't know. If it be God's will ..." She runs her fingertips along her gold neck chain and rubs the cross.

Max bites his lip. He isn't much into religion himself, but he knows Sarah has strong leanings, though he's unsure exactly how far or in what way. It was something they could never come to terms with in the past and a big reason why their attempt at romance was short-lived. That and the fact he couldn't figure out how to please her. On any level, sexual or otherwise. She always came across as generally needy, he just didn't know for what. Or from whom. He had to admit, for all the years they've known each other she's still pretty much a blank to him in terms of who she was and what she wants.

He draws a cigarette from a half-empty pack, lights up and inhales. Sarah watches with genuine curiosity. Max quit smoking over five years ago.

"There's no smoking here, y'know? It's a law," Sarah says.

"Yeah? So, call a cop."

There have been no incidents of flying wheels for four straight days. The crowd's mood has definitely soured. Previous feelings of gaiety have turned to gloom; in some cases, anger. To make things worse, it's August and the temperature is sitting in the high twenties to low thirties. Adults scream at each other, parents scream at children, children scream at pets. Fights break out for no particular reason. Close quarters and poor sanitation practices result in the air being filled with an acrid stench. Garbage is piled everywhere attracting flies and rats. People are literally walking in their own urine and feces. The natives are getting restless. There is a general attitude that something major must occur soon one way or another, pro or con, otherwise murder, bloody murder.

And it does.

At the crossroads of the Allen Express and the 401 a lone woman appears. She's dressed in rags, her head is shaved and her forehead is smeared with a cross of ashes. She speaks to the throng using a police bullhorn. The woman is Sarah Shorter.

"Listen to me," she says, wailing. "God refuses to reveal Himself to you because you have offended Him. You have taken His chosen sacred place and defiled it. There are people here who do not truly believe, but come merely to satisfy their own personal greed. The money changers must be cast from the temple." Sarah grabs the edge of a patio umbrella and topples a hot dog stand. "The merchants must be driven from the sight of God."

She overturns a jewellery case and pulls down a display of souvenir T-shirts adorned with a picture of a giant wheel topped by a halo. Before anyone can react, she upsets a dozen or more other cases containing everything from food to tattoo decals to Tarot cards. Many cheer her actions while most stand by in shocked amazement. Suddenly, a semi roars into view. Arms automatically shoot skyward—pick me, pick me—and everyone freezes to witness the semi's approach. The single body part that moves on any one individual is a set of praying lips.

"Oh my God, oh dear God, oh God, please accept this most wretched creature as the instrument of your great plan ..."

The semi covers ground and disappointment can be read on the faces of those passed by (or passed up, as the case may be) as no wheel detaches to transport someone to the promised land. Sarah allows for no such twist of fate and refuses to wait for the perfect alignment of stars. Instead, she lets out a mighty whoop, dashes onto the highway and throws herself in front of the huge rig. Her body vanishes instantly beneath the rolling wheels. Hundreds of others immediately follow suit, charge from both sides of the highway toward the truck while the driver attempts unsuccessfully to steer clear of the onslaught.

"What the fuck!" he yells. "Get outta the fucking way! Get outta ..."

Too late. By the time he grinds his truck to a halt, at least a dozen bodies lie dead: scattered, bloodied and broken both on the road and blown off to the side, their mouths ripped into grotesque smiles across their faces.

Others are not so fortunate ... they're still among the living.

For thine is the kingdom. One hail Mary, two hail Marys ...

⌒

The sundry religious factions are quick to denounce the dead as radicals and in no way deserving the title of martyr. They had not been chosen, but instead, had succumbed to their own frail vanity. They were simple suicides, weak, confused and human, all too human. The proof of this was self-evident: They were dead and nothing had changed.

With this recognition of the true nature of God's will, the multitudes re-group along the highway more determined than ever to witness the real miracle. It is clear that God will provide in His own way and in His own time.

A more thorough sanitation program is established and put into action. The city provides portable toilets and showers along with frequent and regular garbage pick-up and massive supplies of potable water. Electrical wires are laid and a lighting grid is set up along the roadside complete with outlets for fans and air conditioners. Small stages are constructed. Microphones and amplifiers are plugged in. Music fills the air. Bands set up concerts. The various spiritual leaders tread the boards and spread the word.

The stretch of highway begins to resemble a giant rock concert. Or a church of the holy rollers convention.

Or a bathed-in-neon Las Vegas resort complete with twenty-four hour Cirque du Soleil performances.

People return to their former activities with a vengeance.

⌒

When Max hears of Sarah's death, he turns in his badge.

"There's nothing to be done," he tells himself. "Whatever happens happens and nothing I can do to change a damn thing."

He heads to the nearest bar and orders a double whiskey. He's generally a beer drinker and the first hard shot burns going down. By the second and third, he appears to have the hang of it. He hoists his glass. "Here's to you, Sarah. I hope you found whatever it was you were looking for."

Another week passes with still no sign from above and the crowd again grows restless. Two days pass. A third day more.

Rumours arrive that the trucking companies are cracking down to ensure that no wheel flies off, whether by accident or by design. Neither the owners nor the drivers want trouble. When the devotees hear this, they are outraged, calling the action sacrilegious. They decide to strike back. In the name of God, any truck driving through the holy zone intact would be met at the end, stopped, boarded and dismantled, the parts smashed and tossed in so many different directions that it would make reassembly impossible. They'll teach the Philistines not to interfere with the ways of God.

~~~

Bright early evening and candles continue to burn at the gravesite of James Corrigan. Members of the Legion of the Almighty appear to be bound and determined to wait out the resurrection. Dozens of them stretch out on the grass or lean against gravestones talking, praying, smoking, drinking lemonade or perhaps something stronger. The rumoured Hollywood agent sits on a blanket dealing stud poker and sucking back a highball with a few of the boys. Mrs. Corrigan has made the place rather cheery, draping a picnic table with a red and white checked cloth, providing lawn chairs, replacing the cut flowers regularly, keeping the coffee pot fresh on the Coleman stove. For his part, Mr. Corrigan maintains his position at the BBQ, firing up the grill with burgers, dogs, steaks and chicken. Patio lanterns are strung between the tree branches. A fingernail moon struggles to be noticed as the sun slowly sinks.

The picture is very Norman Rockwell-like.

Onto this bucolic scene stumbles Max. He looks like death warmed over—unkempt, unwashed, unshaven, unpressed. He brandishes a shovel in one hand and a bottle of Canadian Club rye whiskey in the other. At the foot of J.C.'s grave, Max takes a slug of whiskey and begins to dig. No one raises a finger to prevent him. Perhaps no one can believe what they're seeing. Perhaps Max's dissolute image is too frightening. Perhaps they feel that it's time for action—any action—and this man may be here as the implement of God. Perhaps he is, even, the angel Gabriel himself arrived in disguise. More likely though, they're all bored to tears and fed up with waiting.

Bring it on!

Max digs deeper, stopping occasionally to quench his thirst. At one such pause, Mr. Corrigan offers him a burger and potato salad, but Max is too intent on his task to notice. One might say that Max behaves like a man possessed. And he is. Whether by God or the devil is unclear.

Men and women rise from the grass and inch closer toward the grave.

When Max reaches the coffin, he uses the shovel to pry open the lid. Therein lies James Corrigan, stuffed to the gills with formaldehyde, his wounds covered in garish make-up, still looking decidedly dead. Maxwell leans in for a better view. He sighs, grunts, polishes off the remaining whiskey, tosses the empty bottle aside, grabs the stiff body by the starched white collar and hauls its sorry ass to the surface. Everyone backs away. There is a hush as Max deposits the ragged body at the feet of the crowd. They stand dumbfounded. Max wipes some dirt from his lips and studies the mutilated dead thing on the ground before him.

"I give you your redeemer," he mumbles. He turns and staggers off into the night. As he disappears, someone attempts to speak. It's Mrs. Corrigan. Her mouth opens, her jaw works, her throat quavers. That's it. That's all she can muster. There are no words forthcoming. She stops and shakes her head. The crowd disperses a few at a time. Mr. Corrigan shuts the BBQ lid and turns off the propane tank. The Hollywood agent picks up his valise, rattles out the key to his rental car as he heads down the cobblestone path.

Gerry sees Max enter the bar and motions him over. "Buy you a drink?" he asks.

"Yeah," Max says. "A ginger ale."

Max looks good. His hair is cut, he's clean, his clothes are ironed and he's shaved.

"Sorry about Sarah," Gerry says. "I didn't get a chance to tell you. You disappeared. You OK?"

"Yeah, I'm OK." Max sips his ginger ale. "So, what happened to everyone?"

"*Poof!* Scattered."

"Howcum?"

"You don't know?"

Max shrugs. "I've been kinda outta touch."

"Flying wheels suddenly started appearing all over the place — Calgary, Vancouver, Paris, Rome, Tokyo, Los Angeles — you name it. It was in my column."

"Is it true?"

Gerry gives Max a look. "Are you kidding me?"

"So, why'd you write it?"

"The story was dead here. No one was buying it

anymore. Companies refused to send their trucks in; business put heat on the politicians; politicians put heat on the cops ..."

"Cops put heat on the press."

"Bingo."

"And they believed you?"

"It's the newspaper, pal. It's like gospel."

"Yeah, I guess." Max nods. "And what happens when these fine folk travel to places unknown and figure out they've been duped?"

"Oh, you know ... always somewhere else to go, something else to discover and go crazy over—Mother Theresa's face in a sesame bagel or image of the Virgin Mary on a shower stall wall or crying ceramic elephants or ..."

"Right, right."

The two stare at the TV. Gerry lets out a muffled laugh.

"So, give," Max says, turning.

"It's nothing, really."

"Yeah?"

"Yeah. It's just that, as soon as everyone split for greener pastures, there was a wheel-off on the 401, near Kennedy."

"Yeah?"

"Yeah. And today there was one at the Don Valley."

"You gonna print it?"

Gerry makes a face. "It's just another wheel-off, right? Happens all the time. Where's the story in that?"

The two grin and raise their glasses.

"Cheers," Gerry says. He places a hand on Max's shoulder. "To Sarah."

They nod and return their attention to the screen. It's the bottom of the seventh and the Jays are losing to the Angels. The two men are silent. They sip their drinks. They grin. Somehow, everything fits.

THE ONLOOKER'S TALE

"I don't like Mondays. This livens up the day."
—*Brenda Ann Spencer*

In which a seemingly innocent pastime
on a warm sunny summer day
somehow turns gradually violent.

A weekday. I should be somewhere. Doing something. Where? What? School, maybe. That's the ticket. Earn that diploma that promises future so bright gotta wear shades. Yeah, baby! Or on the job, putting my skills to proper use, fulfilling my obligation as a role model and responsible citizen, raking in real dough along with paid vacations, pension plan, my own personal key to the company john and a little something on the side. Sweet. Mebbe hangin' out on da porch wit ma and pa over a pitcher o'cold lemonade fixin' ta do chores around da ole homestead: collect eggs from da cows, milk da chickens, plow da paved back forty wit da Beamer, yee-hah! In choich, accountin' for me sins to the holy ghost-lies: one Tequila, two Tequila, three Tequila, floor. Or else sitting my ass down in a coffee shop working on my latest blockbuster screenplay. Sick. Should be. Most definite. Instead. Fuckin' the dog. Drawn by a notion. An urge. What could be simpler?

It's a lovely, warm, summer afternoon, barely a breeze

to whip up a distracting leaf or provoke a disturbing sound. The crowd is orderly, well-behaved, comprised of the usual: men, women, children in strollers, dogs on leashes. They wear sun hats, sun glasses, shorts, T-shirts, thin blouses, sandals. They reek a combination sun tan lotion (coconut, cocoa butter) and bug spray. Cameras hang from necks, though expectations are low in terms of actual worthwhile photo-ops arising. More for show. Or habit. Hot dogs and fries from the chip wagons are being consumed along with ice cream bars, giant Slurpees, Cokes, take-out coffees. Cigarettes are smoked.

Away from the action, off to the sides, not so much "ordered to" as "requested by" the hired security, down-at-heel panhandlers ply their trade. The odd derelict drinks from a concealed bottle. A couple of pals pass a joint. No big whoop. Pigeons, sparrows and gulls bide time for whatever scraps fall from cardboard trays, so that, even here, at the fringes, exists an atmosphere of calm, polite civility. What's that stupid joke? How do you get a crowd of Canadians out of the swimming pool? Say: "Would you please get out of the swimming pool."

No one in a hurry. They stroll; they amble; they *mill*. A place for everyone and everyone in their place. They are perfectly suited, perfectly prepared for the scheduled event. *Non*-event, really. A truck stop at Nathan Phillips Square. One of many across the country in advance of an election. Mouth a litany of hollow words. Kiss a few hands, shake a few babies. That sort of thing. Blah-blah-blah. Smile, wave, move inside city hall to share further lies with the local politicos. Hardly worth the bother, the expense, yet, there it is. Pomp and circumstance. Bread and circuses. When you can't offer anything of substance to the people, pacify them with a parade.

Not that anyone's dissatisfied today. They aren't. You'd expect at least one token placard: Save The Whales, Abolish Abortion, Stop The Pipeline. Something. Anything. Instead, nada. Everyone happy happy.

There are uniformed police, of course, but they're only present as *part-of-the-job*, appearing outwardly relaxed, leaning against low wire fences, their revolvers holstered, strapped, safeties on, sharing small talk, nudging elbows, telling a joke or two, laughing discreetly. Their entire conduct evidences unconcern. One middle-aged cop with a paunch yawns into a hand. Maybe he's working a double shift, scoring some easy OT so he can take the little woman to Casino Rama on the weekend, get their freak on with the *Kiss* tribute band. "Gonna rock and roll all nite and party everyday." Is that tongue fer real or a strap-on, d'y'think? Or play the slots. Or maybe it's dinner and a movie. Hit the Mandarin for Chinese buffet. Catch the latest asinine Apatow or whatever other drunken rom/com. Have a few yuks, hope there's a bit of girlish T&A alongside the ubiquitous chubby funnyman's hairy butt shenanigans. The possibilities for mediocrity being endless, there's no lack of fun times if you're orally fixated, emotionally challenged and/or clinically brain dead.

There are likely a number of undercover types as well prowling the vicinity though this precaution too would have less to do with a perceived threat than for reasons of protocol, tradition and the normal employment of bureaucratic procedures. Red tape and the like. Dotting 'tees' and crossing 'eyes' and so on. Just as the private bodyguards presiding on the small makeshift stage are there strictly for show. A flex of muscle. After all, beyond the usual (and expected) amount of low grumblings, odd booing, rarer tomato or cream pie toss, there is little to record in the way of actual violence at one of these affairs, low key or otherwise. Bruises certainly, a splash of blood here and there, admittedly, broken bones once in a while, understandably, though all of this among the crowd, not involving the dignitaries themselves who are generally tucked well out of harm's way. To be honest, when there was violence it tended to occur in the pubs following, not during the official proceedings.

The bodyguards, in truth, look to have grown lackadaisical, off-hand, maybe even bored with their occupation. And who can blame them? In the entire Canadian political landscape there has never been a Prime Minister assassinated. Very few even died in office and most lived reasonably long lives after their terms in that position. "Oh, Canada, we stand on guard." Those telling words. "We stand on guard." Cooling our heels. Off-stage. Out of the limelight. Standing on guard. Waiting. Forever waiting.

How different from the good old US of A and its LAND OF THE FREE, HOME OF THE BRAVE lyric sung in bold letter caps and tattooed on the brain. The good old US of A with its right to bear arms and a bent to enter any fray with both guns blazing, no questions raised, no response required, no apologies necessary. No quarter asked, none given. The good old US of A where there have been four presidents assassinated with more than twenty further failed attempts and countless other rumoured attempts. Not to mention copycats down-the-line gaining headlines with their own private brand of mass assassination covering thirty states from Massachusetts to Hawaii, twenty-five since 2006, at: a nursing home in North Carolina, an elementary school in Connecticut, a Sikh temple in Wisconsin, a theatre in Colorado, an IHOP in Nevada, a health spa in California, a café in Seattle—nowhere safe from anyone diagnosed armed and dangerous and little understanding why.

"The silicone chip inside her head gets switched to overload and nobody's gonna go to school today." Boomtown Rats riff on the old tune: up shit creek without a paddle and no one taking much notice, say, of a young girl perched in a third story window overlooking a quiet playground in San Diego, California.

Not that someone earlier hadn't seen signs, suspected and tried to intervene—even recommended the girl be admitted to a psychiatric hospital—but her father stubbornly refused, and for Christmas gave her a Ruger 10/22 semi-automatic .22 calibre rifle with a telescopic sight and 500 rounds of ammunition.

She'd asked for a radio.

"Sweet sixteen ain't that peachy keen … they can see no reasons, 'cos there are no reasons."

How do you get a crowd of Canadians out of the swimming pool?

The bodyguards go through the motions, patrol the stage, tap their earphones, adjust their sunglasses, straighten their skinny black ties: ten-four, ten-four. Whatever. Their minds are on other things. Grocery lists, laundry lists, plans for the weekend, the nice meal that goes with the job at the end of the day, red wine or white, what they'd do if they won a million in the lottery. A female bodyguard cleans an ear with an index finger and wipes it on a tissue. She uses a file on her fingernails. A male bodyguard has his binoculars trained across Queen Street: balcony of a suite in the Sheraton Hotel. There's a skinny woman with sunk cheeks and a pointy nose wearing a tan-coloured leisure suit framed in the window, holding the drapes apart with spread arms, checking out the square. Perhaps the guard is undressing the woman in his mind. Perhaps he's screwing her from behind doggie-style; perhaps he's already screwed her; perhaps he's prancing around her room sporting a platinum blonde wig, garish make-up, a pink lace bra, pink thong panties and a pair of black stiletto heels; perhaps he's lying in a pool of blood, the sharp heel of one shoe imbedded in his eye, through his brain; perhaps he's saying to himself: I'd kick her out of bed for eating crackers but I wouldn't let her off the floor, har-har. Impossible to know for sure, there's just that *feel* to the scene.

And so it is with the rest of the bodyguards, the police, the suits, the hired help, the crowd as well— here and not here; excited yet not; involved though so-so; interested while not giving two shits one way or the other. Merely something to do to pass the time and a beautiful day to be out, whether the PM arrives or not, and a million other things going through their heads at the same time. And me too, me too, as I am part of the crowd and also separate from the crowd, going about my business anonymously: unchecked, unnoticed, ignored.

How simple it would be, I think, given the situation, the surroundings, the circumstances. Imagine, an anonymous crowd attending an anonymous event? What better time? Wait for the PM to stand at the microphone. Wind through the crowd until you are directly in front and within a few yards of said target. There's no one to stop you. Everyone is caught up in their own thoughts. Standing guard. Waiting.

So be it.

Withdraw a revolver from a deep pocket, a medium-sized purse or tote sack, a zippered backpack compartment, a plain brown paper bag, raise it swiftly to eye level, aim and fire. Empty the cartridge in rapid succession. *Boom, boom, boom!* Watch the PM jerk spastically on the platform as the bullets hit. The whole thing lasts maybe two or three seconds at most. The PM drops heavily to the ground. There's an instant of shocked immobility by everyone present, followed by the sharp, almost painful, recognition of the truth of what has just occurred and, finally, the inflamed reaction around these events. Heads turn, cameras and cell phones are fumbled to faces as if a thousand Zapruders called upon to record for posterity, THE ACT. Black suited bodies fly through the crowd, shoving and pushing, brandishing handguns and billy clubs, there are gasps and screams and shouts, people wail and cry. Numerous rough hands work to pin the arms and legs of the assailant to the pavement. There are solid, punishing blows delivered to the downed face and body.

I feel those blows, feel those rough hands grabbing and tearing at me.

What else? I see the revolver. I see the fist holding the revolver. I see *my* fist holding the revolver. I see my fist raising the revolver to eye level, aiming the revolver at the Prime Minister, pulling the trigger. I hear the shots fire. *Boom, boom, boom!* I feel the cartridge empty. I see the body jerk spastically and drop heavily to the ground. I smell the burn of gunpowder and see the final trace of smoke exit the barrel. Next, in order: the Zapruder cameras, the flying suits, the rough hands pinning me to the pavement, the solid, punishing blows to my face and body, the sight of a dozen puzzled question marks twisted on a dozen broad foreheads.

Horse out of the gate and hindsight being 20/20, Boomtown Rats nail it all the way to the bank: "What reason do you need to die?"

What reason indeed?

"This livens up the day."

I'd asked for a radio.

Would you please get out of the pool? Please? Please?

THE STALKER'S TALE

In which a woman becomes the unwitting object of desire and intimate study by an un-named, unidentified and unreliable narrator.

He waits for her to get off work. Plants himself on the busy street corner propped against a government mail box, one arm curled over top, the other bent at his side, hand hooked in his jacket pocket, back curved, shoulders hunched. The short beard hairs on his jaw scrape a bare knuckle of the free hand. He eases a cell phone from the jacket pocket and checks the time. Any minute now. He tucks the cell phone away. His head bobs to a tune pulsing through a set of ear buds: "Crazy mama, where you been so long ..." He mouths the words. "Crazy mama ..." J.J. Cale, he thinks. Rock on, mother-fucker. "Crazy mama ..." He shifts the position of his legs. Any minute now.

A few things he knows: her name, where she works, her line of employment, how much she earns per hour, her social insurance number, her bank balance, where she lives, who she lives with, where she shops, her age, her birthday, the fact that Tuesday night is movie night, Wednesday night is Pilates, every other weekend or so is the train ride to Guelph to visit mom and pop, that she has recently stopped eating red meat, gone organic, her laundry soap is eco max, she's allergic to cats—which is a big drag 'cause sometimes she thinks she'd like to have a cat, oh well. Other more personal (even *intimate*) information includes: her dress size, her shoe size, her bra size, the fact she listens to Country Western music, dyes her hair, drinks dry white wine, irons her underwear, has a rose tattoo on her belly just below the navel, keeps a box of Trojan lubricated ribbed condoms in the night table beside her bed 'just in case,' also a vibrator with dying batteries. And that she weeps when she masturbates.

There's more. Much more. He rubs the tips of his fingers together and gives them a sniff. He tugs his beard. "Crazy mama ..."

And there she is, right on schedule. She descends the stairs, pushes through the glass doors into the crisp autumn air. She stops momentarily, gazes up for signs of rain, weather reports having indicated. There's a bank of rolling dark clouds and that's it. Perhaps later, overnight. She gives her hat a slight tug, adjusts her shoulder bag and makes her way along the sidewalk. He drifts casually behind, not so much ogling as studying her.

No great shakes, really, if you tend to judge by current Hollywood standards. Five foot four in heels. Chunky legs. Wide hips. A bit broad in the beam. Could afford to lose a few pounds. Wait a minute—who said that? Someone. Words in a song. No. "... a little too tall, coulda used a few pounds." Bob Seger. *Night Moves*. Different thing altogether. Whatever. Something in the way of tits, though nothing remarkable here either. What do they say?

More than a mouthful's a waste? Maybe. Thin lips, largish somewhat pointed nose, narrow eyes, troubled skin masked by foundation, conditioner and rouge. To be completely frank and honest, overly made up. Lipstick, eye liner, mascara, powder and so on. Blame the job. Otherwise, luck of the draw. That, and the infernal gene pool. At any rate, nothing to write home about from any vantage point. Not that he's anywhere near a prize catch himself. He's not. Not by a long shot. Not that any of this matters. It doesn't. What matters is, they have each other.

"When you're given lemons, make lemonade." He believes this.

She turns left off Yonge onto Isabella. He hovers at a distance. A safe distance. No chance he'll lose her. She'll march into Rabba's Fine Foods and grab something to nuke for dinner: a small vegetarian pasta or casserole dish. There are salad fixings in the fridge. Plus a bottle of chilled white wine, a gift from her parents during her last visit. The wine is Narcissist Riesling purchased at the aptly named Megalomaniac winery. The parents had recently returned from a bus tour in the Niagara region. They figured she'd get a chuckle. They did. They also hoped she'd like the wine: clear, pale, straw colour, floral and peach aromas with a touch of lemon. She'd have to let them know. He hopes she'll crack it tonight. He expects she will. She isn't what some might call a heavy drinker, enjoying a glass or two each night, perhaps more over a weekend or at a party, though she does sometimes worry if she shouldn't cut back. A glass at least tonight, with dinner, if only to report back to the parents, as they've been asking. Followed by a curl up with a fat romance novel and a shower before heading off to bed. She had been well into one such novel—one which he was really quite enjoying—when she suddenly slapped it shut and tossed it into the recycling bin. No reason given, which had him scratching his head. He retrieved it, finished it on his own and still can't comprehend what the problem was as it read like countless other romance novels she'd begun and always completed in the past, cover to cover.

She approaches the register. The cashier behind the counter hits a few keys, says go ahead, she inserts her debit card chip first into the machine. "I-M-1-2," the man outside goes as she punches in the pin number. The transaction goes through. The woman exits the store and walks east toward her apartment, the man dogging her. He weaves in and out of darkened doorways, alleyways, store fronts. He fancies himself a shadow among shadows. Invisible and silent. Right. She enters her building, crosses the carpeted floor of the lobby, presses the elevator button. He huddles outside the window, waits and watches as she disappears behind the sliding doors. Second floor, he goes. Third floor, fourth floor. Down the hall. Room 404. Key in the handle. Turn the key. Push the handle, remove the key, kick the door shut with her heel.

Now, where's that white wine, hmm? Slip out of her shoes and pad barefoot to the fridge. Ah, yes.

She's at work early the next morning after a quick breakfast of coffee, high fibre cereal, almond milk, lo-fat yogurt and a banana. The banana eating always gets to him, despite Freud's "sometimes a banana is just a banana" dictum. He doesn't know why, it just does. The evidence rests scattered on the synthetic granite countertop: empty Tassimo disc, empty yogurt container, spoon, bowl, banana peel. She sips at a second coffee grabbed along the way and stored on a shelf behind the display counter. Cosmetic department of the Bay. She rubs a spray of perfume between her wrists.

He roams the apartment bold as a brass balled monkey, as his good old mother used to say, god-rest-her-soul. Does she have any idea he's there? The woman? Any inkling? Why should she? When she left the apartment she locked the door and that was that. Or so she thought. How did he get in? A limited number of possibilities include: the front door, the balcony door, the bathroom window; he used a key, he jimmied the lock with a credit card, a hairpin, the metal clip from a ballpoint pen; he crawled through the ventilation shaft, the heating duct, a hole in the wall, a secret passage; he smuggled himself inside the hollowed-out form of a large wooden horse; he slipped through a fissure, a crack; voodoo magic, sleight-of-hand, telekinesis ... whatever. He's in. That's what counts.

He surveys the scene. There's the usual disarray. Delicate, hand-washed personal items drip-dry over the curtain rod. A damp terrycloth towel hangs from a hook on the wall. Glass and plastic make-up containers, cotton balls, Q-Tips, foam applicators, mix and mingle with vitamins, dietary supplements, sprays and tubes, waxed peppermint flavoured dental floss, the torn paper wrapper from a Tampon on the porcelain sink. A few drops of menstrual blood stain the white floor tiles. He touches everything. Picks objects up. Shakes them. Sniffs them. Bites them. Licks them. Puts them back. He doesn't worry about fingerprints. Or DNA. Why should he? He's not a criminal. He fingers his iPod. Settles on The Hip: "New Orleans is sinking and I don't wanna swim."

The toilet bowl and tub are in need of a good scrub, a chore generally reserved for the weekend. She didn't flush earlier, not wanting to waste water. He unzips, urinates in the bowl, careful not to drip on the rim. The mirrored door of the medicine cabinet is partially open. Same goes for the vanity and chest drawers in the bedroom which reveal glimpses of underwear, socks and sweaters. Further articles of clothing cover the bedspread, indicating a decision-making process around what to wear today. Or not. Shoes and boots litter the floor, either singly or in pairs. There is the already mentioned breakfast mess in the kitchen. He opens the fridge and sees she didn't replace the screw top on the bottle. Too bad. The wine was very tasty, though he did fail to experience the advertised aroma of peach and touch of lemon. Would she notice if he was to put in a stopper?

He tugs a pair of black thong underwear from his pants pocket and twirls it around his index finger. *Butt floss*, he smiles. She never seems aware when any of these items go missing. Simply waits for the next sale and buys more. Or if her watch moves from the bedside table to the living room coffee table. Or her shoulder bag from the hall to slung over a kitchen chair. Or her cell phone which she knows damn well she returned to her bag and which she eventually discovers in her coat pocket or hidden part way under the couch or on a window sill. Or her gloves. Things like that which are simply part and parcel of everyday clutter, and so, susceptible to memory lapses, Freudian slips, brain farts and general confusion due to over-stimulated gray matter. Soup to nuts and where is that lovely lilac knitted wool scarf with the purple and gold-patterned weave I know it was in this drawer? Where indeed? Not to worry, it'll turn up somewhere, eventually. Still, annoying at the time and a puzzle that eats away at the back of the brain.

The wine stopper is a whole other kettle of fish that bears considerable consideration. Pros and cons and so on. Benefits and risks. Give and take. To be or not to be. *Rouge et Noir.* Sartre's Existential Angst visible in the minutest detail, prepared, as ever, to come back and bite you in the ass. The more things change the more they remain the same, all right. Comforting. Solace as well in Ortega y Gasset's: "The fundamental biological nature of man and human consciousness has not changed since the late Palaeolithic times." Woo-hoo! A time we drove the fabulous woolly mammoth plus other Pleistocene Megafauna to extinction through human disease and over-hunting. Old habits being hard to break, yes? Also a time of growing leisure and the genesis of Art, Music and Religion. The famed carved figurine *Venus of Willendorf* epitomizing the pursuit of the mother goddess. Also pornography. Also cannibalism. He (our protagonist) isn't aware of any of this, of course. His *modus operandi* is based solely on primal urges and gut instincts.

You is strictly from hunger, pal! No shit Sherlock.

"Ain't got no picture postcards, ain't got no souvenirs ..."

He returns the thong underwear to his pants pocket, opens a drawer and fishes out a rubber stopper with a pewter top in the shape of a lizard. She used to collect this sort of thing—reptiles and other amphibious creatures—plaster frog doorstop, metal snake bookmark, wooden alligator bookends, jade dragon earrings, crazy popular photo of that Mexican woman with the several iguanas on her head. Not so much anymore. Grew tired, he guesses. He shoves the stopper into the neck of the bottle and shuts the fridge.

He stares at the front door. He imagines her walking in on him at this exact moment. Home early from work. A headache, maybe. Maybe cramps due to her period. Blood stains on the floor. Catching him there. Red handed. His first thought? "I'm a shadow among shadows, invisible and silent." Nice try. She ain't buying. She shoots him a look, like: Who are you? What are you doing here? How did you get in? The usual questions.

He's dressed in a sheer silver bareback teddy. The narrow straps are tight and dig into his shoulders and chest. Stuffed wads of Kleenex offer a semblance of breasts. There's an obvious oblong-shaped bulge in the crotch. His feet overfill a pair of black high-heeled pumps.

He sports a blonde wig, false eyelashes, rouged cheeks, a slash of cherry red lipstick and silver hoop earrings engraved with tortoise outlines.

She appears calm in the face of it; reaches for the hem of her skirt, raises it above her calf, above her knee, reveals a pink holster strapped to her thigh. She withdraws a small revolver and points it in the man's direction. The revolver fits her hand perfectly. It's a .22 or a .38 or a .45. It's a 9mm Browning automatic. Or a Glock 19 semi-automatic. He knows nothing about handguns nor what the well-armed woman packs these days in terms of heat. He seems to recall hearing that a .357 Magnum high impact snubbie is a popular choice for a woman these days, though he can't be sure.

What's your game, buster? Do I call the cops or plug you where you stand? Make like a canary and sing before I fill you fulla lead.

She uses words and phrases like this: "game," "buster," "plug," "cops," "make like a canary and sing," "fulla lead." Dialogue right out of an old *film noir*. He has to admit, it's pretty sexy and he wonders if it's true, that when a man dies violently, he ends with an erection? He can't deny a certain amount of excitement building *down there* even as she licks her lips, cocks the hammer and squeezes off a few rounds.

"My memory is muddy, what's this river that I'm in? New Orleans is sinking and I don't wanna swim, yeow!"

She enters the apartment, kicks off her shoes, hangs her jacket and bag on a hook in the hallway, crosses to the kitchen. The man freezes.

"I'm a shadow among shadows," he thinks. "Invisible and silent."

She drops a Styrofoam carton of food on the counter, opens the fridge, removes the wine from the door, grabs a glass and sets these items next to the carton. She stares at the stopper in the bottle. She doesn't remember putting it in last night, though she must have. She remembers the twist top wouldn't snap and she had to cut and pry it off with a paring knife. It was totally mangled and useless and she tossed it in the garbage. It only makes sense she put in the stopper. From inside the Styrofoam carton she rips a large BBQ rib and chews and sucks it clean. She drops the bone in the lid and licks her fingers. She carries her glass to the couch and curls up in the corner with her legs tucked under her. She picks up her book and opens it at the spot where she placed the metal snake bookmark. She sips her wine. Nice, she thinks. Floral and peach aromas with a touch of lemon.

He kneels on the floor beside her, his body pressed against the arm of the couch: "a shadow among shadows; invisible and silent." Cat-like, he nuzzles her shoulder to get a closer view of the book. It's a slim novel, Don DeLillo's *The Body Artist*. He reads along with her: "She thought of a man showing up unexpectedly. Not the man who was here now. Another man. It was nothing, it was something that came into her mind while she ate her breakfast, a man appearing suddenly, as in a movie ..."

It was beginning to get interesting.

THE CRIMINALS' TALE

"There is no trap so deadly as the trap you set for yourself."

—*Raymond Chandler*

In which a group of petty criminals devises a foolproof plan to kidnap a star football player, only to discover the snatch is fraught with circumstances outside their experience and beyond their control.

Four of them met in a rented private room in the basement of Clinton's Pub on Bloor Street. The space was old, dim, dingy, even dirty, sparsely furnished, with evidence of more than a few pitchers of beer and ashtrays spilled on the carpet over the years and the men preferred it that way. A favoured spot where they were allowed to smoke cigars, drink scotch and talk without either interruption or interference. They were of a similar age—mid to late fifties—sporting ties and jackets, and carried with them that sort of been there, done that, bought-the-T-shirt attitude that comes with having achieved a certain level of monetary success. One of them held court while the others listened.

"With the win last night, the Argos have clinched

first place in the east, that means they get a bye until the semi-finals in two weeks. Am I correct in saying this?" The others motioned and murmured a sort of tacit agreement. "Which means, we have a relatively short period of time to strategize and initiate a plan of action. To this end, I put the question to you: Who is the most valuable player to the team?"

"Gotta be the QB, what's'isname?" Vincent snapped his fingers a couple of times. "Mankowski or somethin'."

"Manikowski, I think. Yeah, it's always the QB," Sid said.

John rocked his head and surveyed the table. "What about you, Anthony? Do you know who the quarterback is for the Toronto Argonauts?" Anthony took a breath and blew through his lips, no. "It's a black kid named Romero," John said. "Second stringer barely gettin' by after Marcuzzi went out a month ago with a broken collar bone." The other three nodded like it was news they maybe vaguely remembered, though not really.

"Running back, then," Vincent said. "Pierce, or someone, right?"

"Close. Pearson. Having a pretty good year, but not stellar. Anyone else?" No one spoke. John sighed. "Do you guys know anything about the team?"

"I gotta say, I don't really watch CFL. I'm a Bills' fan," Sid said.

"Yeah, Steelers." That was Vincent.

"Lakers," Anthony said. The others gave him the old hairy eyeball. "Hey, football's too fucking slow. All that huddling and whatnot. Buncha pussies. Takes half an hour to play the final two minutes, gimme a break." He poked the air with his cigar.

"OK, fine," John said. "Just to catch you up so we're on the same fucking page, yes? The Argos have currently won twelve out of eighteen games and of these twelve, only three were by eight points or more, the rest by less than six and ten of these were decided in the final four minutes or in OT, generally by a field goal. What does that tell you?"

"They've been damn lucky," Vincent said, laughing.

"Uh-huh. And what does it tell you about who's been scoring points and winning games for them in pressure situations?" John topped up his glass and relit his cigar. The others passed the bottle in turn.

Anthony threw his hands open in the air. "The kicker?"

"The kicker, exactly. Name of Larry Donovan. Thing is, he's also the punter, which is rare these days, in an era of specialization. Leads the league not only in field goals, but in dropping kicks inside the ten, which makes him extra valuable. Take him out of the mix and the Argos have squat."

"So, that's who we snatch."

"Yeah. The real beauty part is that his place of residence is a downtown hotel. The Sheraton. He's single, lives alone and has no family to speak of. It's like he's begging for it."

"How do you know all this?" Vincent asked.

"Fucking Google, man! Just hit a button," John said, grinning. "There's just one slight hitch. Where do we keep him after we've made the snatch? My new apartment building's so secure, they got cameras watching the cameras."

"Not my place. The wife and I just downsized. She'd have a fit. What about you, Sid? You've got a basement suite that's free."

"*Had* a basement suite. My daughter split from her asshole husband—finally—and moved in with her two kids. No way."

"Vincent! You've got the heated garage in Parkdale. It's perfect."

"Sure, it's always left up to the black brother, right? Except that heated garage is storing a shit-load of TVs you guys were supposed to move over six months ago. I barely got room to park my vehicle never mind hide a fucking Argonaut."

"Look," John said. "We'll come by with the truck and clear out the TVs, OK? Put 'em in a rental unit or something. Worse comes to worse, we each take a few sets home and give 'em away as Christmas gifts."

"Everyone I know already has a TV in every room."

"Yeah, and no one wants a thirty-two inch anymore, anyway."

"Whatever. We figure it out later."

"Fine. And what if the guy wants to take a piss or something? There's no facilities in the garage."

"Speaking of which ..." Sid let out a loud fart, and pointed a finger to the ceiling. "Ducks," he said. The men laughed.

"Nice one," John said. "Anyway, give him a bucket.

It ain't the Sheraton, right? With any luck, he won't be there long anyway. Face it, without him, the Argos got no chance in hell even getting a sniff of the Grey Cup." John raised his glass. "We clear?"

"Clear," the others repeated.

"Good. Let's get to work."

They hunkered in to listen as John went over details.

Three of the men stationed themselves in various locations of the hotel lobby and studied a downloaded headshot of Donovan. Vincent was the first to spot him. He signalled the others and followed Donovan up the escalator to his room. The decision had been to tail him a couple of days, see where he hung out and figure the best spot to make the grab. Vincent punched his cell.

"Got him. I'll make myself at home up here and if he steps out I'll let you know. Be ready to pull the car around. Let's hope he's not the type to drink a warm glass of milk and hit the sack early."

Two hours later, around 9:30 p.m., Vincent caught sight of the door crack open. He bent down to tie a lace, realized he was wearing slip-ons and gave his cuffs a quick brush. A woman stepped into the hall. She had platinum blond hair, bright red lips and dark eye lashes so long and thick they could've passed for a set of venetian blinds. She wore a tight red sequined dress cut well below the neck, well above the knees, black fishnet stockings and silver platform heels along with the obligatory pearl necklace, earrings, bracelets and matching silver and pearl encrusted clutch purse.

Holy shit, Vincent thought, as the woman sashayed past him toward the elevator. He made the call downstairs.

"Tell Anthony to get the car. Keep your eyes peeled for a cherry red $500-a-night hooker, and don't lose sight."

"Why we chasin' a skirt?"

"Let's just say I got a hunch this skirt ain't no lady."

"What makes you say?"

"Number one, she looks like she fell off an amateur stage set of *Sweet Charity*. Number two, I think I got a pretty good shot of Adam's apple when she walked by."

"Are you tryin' to tell me ...?"

"I don't know. I'm just sayin', let's follow up and see."

The woman jumped into a cab and the men followed her along Queen and up Church Street.

"Wha'd'y'know," Sid said. "The gay fucking ghetto. Can you believe it? Fucking Argonaut."

The cab stopped and let the woman out. She skipped across traffic into Woody's Bar. Anthony pulled in and parked the SUV.

"Fucking unbelievable," Sid said. "What do we do?"

"Coffee and donuts," Vincent said. "We wait. Maybe we get lucky."

~

She was tied to a chair in the middle of the garage floor under a bank of fluorescent lights. Sid straddled a second chair, leaned his arms across the back, stared at her as she slowly came to. Vincent stooped over the back of another chair nearby. John entered from the side door and cocked his head.

"What's this?" he said.

"This," Sid said, gesturing with a turned palm, "is your superstar Argonaut punter field goal kicker. Bagged and tagged." Vincent sidled over, grabbed a mitt full of hair, raised the blonde wig a few inches and dropped it.

"No shit?" John said.

"Guy's a tranny," Vincent said. "Maybe a fudgepacker. Also ..." Vincent dumped the clutch purse, revealing a used syringe among the make up, plastic credit cards, hotel passkey, bills, change and a half-used roll of mixed Lifesavers. "A junkie. Goes to show, you can't judge a book by its cover."

"I'm not a junkie, you fucking asshole."

"It lives. It speaks," Sid said.

"I'm a diabetic."

"Yeah, and I'm the Queen of England," Vincent said, laughing.

"That your pathetic attempt at a sexist joke?"

"If the shoe fits," Vincent said.

"OK, enough." John motioned to Vincent. "Come with me, we'll make the call." He took a final peek at Donovan and shook his head. "Un-fucking believable," he said. The two men left.

Donovan squinted across at Sid. "You boys getting ready for Hallowe'en, or what?" Sid just sat there, confused. "The Lone Ranger masks." Donovan indicated with his chin.

"This is what's known in the business as a disguise, smart ass." Sid pulled at the corner of his mask and gave it a flick.

"Ooh, impressive! And I suppose you've invented clever little nicknames for yourselves as well, like, Mr. Brown, Mr. Blue, Mr. Pink, yes? So I won't recognize the three of you in a police line-up, is that it?" Donovan beamed at the man, then let out a laugh. "You've been watching way too many bad movies, my friend, if you believe that cheap, thin, piece of black cloth does anything to protect your identity."

"Oh, yeah?" Sid raised his eyebrows and twisted his lips.

"Yeah. Let's start with you. Mid-fifties, I'd say. Thick, curly hair, once dark, now fading to grey. Brown eyes. Five foot eight or nine, one hundred seventy-five pounds, big nose, thick hands and slight accent suggestive of Jewish background. There's a nasal quality to your voice and your breathing is a bit laboured, indicative of a deviated septum. Snorer, for sure. Drives the wife crazy, I bet. Trouble getting a good night's sleep." Donovan leaned his neck and squinted. "Tanned skin in November, nice. You don't appear to be the tanning booth type, so likely recently returned from somewhere hot and sunny. By the sporty windbreaker and brightly patterned polo shirt I'd guess you were golfing, yes?" He paused. "What do you shoot? Mid to high 90s?"

"*Low* to mid 90s."

"Uh-huh. Gold wedding ring with a diamond inset, gold Rolex watch. A knock-off, maybe?"

"It's no knock-off, pal, it's the real thing."

"Real Rolex, fine. Status symbol signifying a man of means. Meanwhile, you wear brown corduroy pants and worn brown size nine or ten Ecco slip on shoes—economical and comfortable. A man of the people."

"Anything else?"

"Left handed."

"How the hell did you know that?"

"You wear your watch on your right wrist. You cross your arms left over right. You tug on your left ear when you're nervous or confused." Donovan paused. "You want me to start on the other two who were just here, or should I go straight to the fourth kidnapper?"

"What fourth kidnapper?"

"Black dude driving the car last night. Similar age to you. Broad-shouldered, heavy-set, bushy salt and pepper hair and beard, Lakers' cap, diamond ear stud, funky John Lennon glasses ..."

"Are you kidding me?"

"I caught a glimpse of him over my shoulder while you and your buddy jumped out of the car and chloroformed me."

"You're a real observant fella. Where'd you learn to do all this?"

"I have a lot of spare time between football seasons. I take courses, one of which was the fine art of police detection, which included detailed observation of clues and characters. Another was Chinese cooking. If you're a good boy, I'll share my recipe for *Baochao yaohua* with you."

"Thanks, I think I'll pass."

"Suit yourself. In the meantime, what's the plan, Mr. Pink?"

"That's funny. You're a funny guy." Sid went to tug his left ear and stopped himself. "Pretty simple. You stay on ice until your team pays the ransom."

"Sounds pretty simple all right. How much are you asking?"

"Three mil."

Donovan leaned back and roared.

"What's so goddamn funny?"

"Do you know anything about the CFL and its pay scale?"

Sid shrugged.

"The cap for the entire team is four million. The average pay per player is about eighty-two grand a year. There's no way anyone is going to pay three million for me."

"If they want a chance at the cup, they'll pay. That's gotta be worth big money. Bonuses and whatever. Incentives."

"I hate to pop your bubble, pal, but the winners of the Grey Cup get sixteen grand apiece, before taxes. The losers, considerably less."

"Sixteen grand? That's it? I gave more than that to my grandson when he was old enough for his bar mitzvah. Are you shittin' me here?"

"Hey, don't shoot the messenger. I'm just sayin'."

"Huh." Sid stared at Donovan. "What about where you're livin'? Can't be cheap holed up at the Sheraton. That's gotta cost money."

"I have a connection. A friend in upper management.

Strictly *quid pro quo*. I could fill in the details, if you're interested."

"It's OK, no need, I get it."

"You're sure?" Donovan put on a pout. "You might get a kick." His ankles were bound to the chair and he only managed to flex his toes for emphasis.

"I'm sure, believe me, I'm sure. Hey—maybe your friend would put up the three mil if the team won't."

"My friend has an expensive wife, three kids he's sending through university and a penchant for betting on the wrong horses. He's in debt up to his balls. Besides, he'd sooner put a bullet through his head than face the possibility of our arrangement becoming public knowledge. Seems to me, you're sucking air on this one, Mr. Pink."

"If what you're telling me is legit, seems like you're the one suckin' air here, pal. And cut with the Mr. Pink, already. If I were you, I wouldn't be makin' jokes. You're in some serious shit."

"Speaking of which, I need to use the toilet. Every morning at this time. Like clockwork." Donovan stared at Sid who reached down between his legs and poked at a small white plastic pail. "I don't think that'll quite cut it, unless you're prepared to slip off my panties, hold me steady and wipe my ass when it's over. Also, I told you I was diabetic. I'm going to need something to eat. And my insulin. Otherwise, Mr. Pink, you're going to have a very sick fella on your hands."

"Insulin'll have to wait. Good chance someone's figured out you're missing by this time. Place'll be buzzin' with cops."

Anthony entered the garage. His bushy hair spilled out from beneath a Lakers' cap. A thin black mask covered his eyes. Around his neck hung a gold chain and pendant. The pendant flashed a garnet coloured letter 'A' on it.

"Hey, Mr. Green! How's it goin'?" Anthony rubbed his hands together and caught Donovan grin and blow Sid a kiss. Sid hung his head and gave a shake.

"Great," Sid said. "Just great." He tugged his ear and pointed to Donovan. "Man needs to use the toilet. Also a sandwich."

"You expect me take him inside the house?"

Sid shrugged. "Unless you got a better idea."

Anthony's eyes passed from the bucket to the man dressed in women's attire and tied to the chair. "Shee-it," he mumbled, as he loosened the ropes and dragged Donovan to his feet.

"And you must be Mr. Black," Donovan said.

"Now, who else would I be?"

Donovan leaned in and gave Anthony a quick sniff. "I just love a man in Old Spice. Makes me want to tear my clothes off and run naked through the woods."

"You keep that thought. Meanwhile, follow me. And no funny stuff. My wife's in a mood and the last thing I need is you provoking her."

"Yeah," Sid said. "And you best put a gunny sack over his head. Otherwise he'll be adding up the change in your pocket. If he hasn't already."

~

Outside the garage, John and Vincent slipped into their masks and barged through the door. They didn't appear any too pleased. Sid and Anthony sat in chairs across from each other, drinking beers and playing Gin Rummy. They used the chair where Donovan sat earlier as a table. Their masks were tucked inside back pockets.

"What the hell goes on?" John asked. "Where's Donovan?"

"Inside," Anthony said. "Don't worry, I've got him cuffed to the radiator." He laid down a card and Sid drew from the pile.

"What's he doin' inside?"

"Started out, take a dump and have a meal. First thing, him and Rosie are redecorating the living room, talking about paint colours and crown mouldings and vintage chintz drapes for the windows and whatnot. Next thing they're exchanging favourite recipes. Now they're cooking up a pot of low-fat chicken tikka masala curry with rice for dinner. It's like they're suddenly BFFs. We couldn't take it anymore and came out here for a beer. How'd it go on your end?"

"It didn't. They put our call through to fucking accounting. Guy said he understood the seriousness of the situation, but the organization's budget didn't cover ransom demands. Best he could offer was tickets to the big game, *if* they made it. Otherwise, he was calling the cops if Donovan wasn't back in uniform and on the field by practice tomorrow."

The four men pondered a moment. Sid jumped in: "What yard line?" he asked. The others shot him a look.

STAN ROGAL

"What? If life serves you lemons, make lemonade, right?" He laughed; the others turned away. "OK, I'm joking. Sue me."

"Probably end zone in the nosebleed section," John said. "I hate dealing with those bean counting asshole bastards. It's like they've got a roll of nickels for a heart."

"So, what do we do?" Sid arranged his cards and set them down in order. "Gin," he said.

Anthony let out a moan and tossed his cards on the chair. Sid totalled the points.

"Maybe we can store him with those TVs we can't unload," Anthony said.

"I say we drop him off where we found him. Cut our losses," Vincent said.

"Makes sense," John said. "You two wore your masks, yeah?"

"Wouldn't matter if we did or didn't. The guy's a regular junior Sherlock Holmes," Sid said.

"What do you mean?"

"He asked me how serious is your arthritis. Figured it might be rheumatoid."

"How did he know that?"

"He noticed the copper bracelets on your wrists. Also, your hands looked puffy and swollen this morning. Saw you rubbing your fingers and stretching your hands to work out the stiffness. Also says you could stand to lose twenty/thirty pounds, it's murder on the knees."

"That it?"

Anthony piped in. "I figure after talkin' with Rosie the past few hours, he knows the names and ages of our kids, grand kids and pets. Probably seen pictures. Wouldn't surprise me if he knew about the heart I've got tattooed on my ass."

"Christ," John said. "That's it, then. He knows too much. We've got no choice."

The men glanced at each other and nodded in unison. A cell phone chimed and Anthony answered. "Yeah? Yeah? Yeah? No!" he said, and hit the off button. "Shit."

"What was that?"

"Rosie. Said Donovan suddenly got faint and passed out on the floor in front of her. She figures it's a diabetic seizure."

"OK, let's get in there! Makes it that much easier for us to dump him."

"Too late. She's in the car, half-way to emergency."

"Thought you said he was cuffed to the radiator?"

"I did. He was." Anthony made a face and shrugged his shoulders. "They're Rosie's cuffs."

⌒

The four men sat in their room at Clinton's, smoking cigars and drinking scotch. There were half-eaten plates of wings, chili nachos and fries spread around the table. They had a small screen TV hooked up to a line that led upstairs. The big game was on. Donovan ran onto the field, prepared to punt from his own thirty. He gave the ball a ride. It took a Toronto bounce and went out of bounds on the Calgary nineteen yard line.

"Sweet," Vincent said.

"Yeah," Sid said, taking a hit of scotch. "Though I can't help but imagine him kicking in that tight red dress and those silver platform heels." The men grunted and laughed.

"Rosie still in touch with him?"

"Oh, yeah. They got the whole Facebook/Twitter thing goin' on," Anthony said. "Wouldn't surprise me if I come home one night and the two of them are cookin' up Szechuan together."

The quarterback for Calgary tossed a screen pass. "Hit him!" Vincent yelled. "Hit him!" The receiver shed two tacklers and gained eighteen yards before being brought down to the turf.

"Buncha pussies," Anthony said. "What did I tell ya?"

John lifted a handful of nachos and scooped out some salsa. "And he never said a word to anyone?" He shovelled the chips into his mouth.

"Hey—'don't ask, don't tell.' This, according to Rosie. Works for me. Business as usual." Anthony joined in the nachos.

"Business as usual. That's good. I like that."

John picked up his cigar and took a few puffs. The others did the same. The Calgary quarterback dropped into the pocket and was blindsided by a blitzing linebacker. The ball popped loose—*fumble*—and was recovered by a Toronto player. The men leapt to their feet and slapped high fives.

Right on, they cheered. Go Argos! They sat down and passed the bottle. Three plays later, Argos drove the ball into the end zone and Donovan came on for the extra point. He split the uprights and the crowd went wild.

"Tight red dress and silver platform heels," Sid said, and gave a low wolf whistle. "Sorry, I can't shake the image."

"Yep," John said grinning. "I hear you." He stretched his hands and gave his fingers a massage. "I think I can safely say we all learned a valuable lesson from this last caper."

"Which is what?" Anthony asked.

"No fucking around with the small stuff. Go big or go home."

"What's that supposed to mean?" Vincent asked.

"What do you think?" John said, inhaling a deep drag from his Corona. "Next time, we kidnap a freaking Raptor."

"Now you're talking," Anthony said. "NBA. Those guys have got shitloads of dough. Probably get three mil for the water boy."

"Then it's settled."

Everyone nodded and murmured enthusiastically in agreement. Sid let out a loud fart and pointed a finger to the ceiling. "Ducks," he said. The men laughed.

Business as usual, John thought. Perfect. He settled back in his chair and re-focused his attention on the game.

Split the uprights and the crowd goes wild.

THE TRAVELLER'S TALE

"There is no excellent beauty that hath not some strangeness in the proportion."
—*Francis Bacon*

In which an actor embarks on a romantic journey that leads him into a realm of make-believe that rivals any stage play an author may have scripted.

While the email appeared substantially less than cryptic, I did scan it several times to be sure I wasn't either reading anything extra into it or else missing something of grave importance that would turn the whole adventure into a wild goose chase. Besides, I found the offer maybe too good to be true, especially as the most the two of us had done was engage in a bit of innocent flirting over craft services while on a film set together in Toronto. That was over six months ago. I was surprised she even remembered me.

The text read: "Hi. I tracked you down through your agent. I had to lie, said it was to do with an audition. Hope you don't mind. My husband is away shooting an action film in the rainforests of Brazil over the next several months. I'm about to go into rehearsals of *Streetcar* for a run in Zurich. I have 7–10 days free before that.

How would you like to come visit me in Switzerland? We have a place in Lenzerheide. September is off-season so no crowds and cheaper air fares. Let me know and we'll work out the details. Sigi."

Now, when I was married—about a hundred years ago it seems— "come visit me" was a euphemism my *ex* used as an invitation for sexual intercourse. I didn't know if it translated in this case or not, though the message was certainly rife with implication. Perhaps the initial flirting wasn't so innocent after all and, to be honest, I would've made a move at the time if she'd given me the slightest indication, which she hadn't. Sigi was about five foot six, solidly built, muscular with dark, short-cropped hair, full lips, thick hands and largish breasts. Not your typical Heidi and I suspected a trace of Gypsy or Latino had jumped the fence somewhere along the hereditary line. She could've passed as a model for a Picasso painting. Combining that with strong acting chops and a Swiss German accent made her sexy as hell. Oh yeah, she also had one green eye and one blue eye which served to make her that much more desirable. Given these traits, I considered: Stella or Blanche in *Streetcar*?

My bank account scraped bottom and not much chance of a major improvement in the foreseeable future. The one bright spot was that my Visa card was clear, though I tried to save this for emergencies. I decided to call a buddy and get his opinion. We met at Pauper's for a beer.

"What's to decide?" he said. "Go, man, go! How

often does this happen? Like, never! The woman is hot and practically throwing herself at you, which I don't understand personally, but makes it all the more imperative. Max out your charge card, sell your first born, knock off a corner grocery store if you have to, but get your ass to Switzerland. You'd be crazy."

It made sense and I appreciated the encouragement.

"It's a no-brainer. There's nothing happening for you here, right?" He drank and blew through his lips. "Sigi Hess, wow!" He rubbed his forehead with a flat palm. "She's gotta be, like, in her late forties, right?"

"Forty-six."

"So, ten years older. Nice. Perfect, in fact. No expectations beyond the act." He grinned and poked my shoulder with his fist. "Lucky bastard. Just don't expect to get hired by her husband if he finds out." He laughed. "I mean, ever."

"Something to consider, for sure. Also, what do I tell my agent?"

"You're going on holiday, what else? It happens, y'know. Actors do take holidays and the business doesn't collapse."

"What if something comes up?"

"You mean, like that call from Scorsese? Why not just buy a ticket for the lottery, you'll have better odds. Face it, you can either stay home and get fucked by your agent, or ... you can go get fucked by Sigi Hess." He performed a balance act with his hands that quickly tipped more one way than the other. Guess which? It was settled. We ordered two more pints. My buddy pulled out his cell phone and started scoping out airline schedules and seat sales.

I landed safely at the Zurich airport. Sigi had told me don't worry, everyone in Switzerland speaks English, you won't get lost, just ask. Well, I did ask, several times, and I had yet to meet anyone who admitted speaking English and finally had to stumble and fumble my way at the local transport ticket booth for directions, which consisted of a series of escalators and ramps and rail lines, any one of which could've ended me in the wrong direction, if not the wrong country. That said, I arrived in downtown Zurich and was met at the train station by an ex-actor pal of mine named Paul. He and his wife Ingrid now worked together in real estate—her chosen profession—both sales and renovations. I'd contacted them ahead of time to see if I could crash at their place for a night, catch up on old times, get the lowdown on Swiss culture, generally have them help me settle in, and next day drop me off and point me in the right direction.

No problem, they replied. It'd be good to see you.

"It's fun," Paul said, speaking of the real estate biz, "and a helluva lot more lucrative than acting."

They had a nice house, a nice couple of kids, two cars, a dog, a cat and were in debt up the wazoo.

"Not a problem unless one of us gets hit by a bus," Paul said, laughing. "It's just the way it is here. Everyone earns a lot and spends more."

Ingrid greeted us at the door and led the way to a pitcher of margaritas in the living room.

"There's a bedroom for you there," she said, motioning. "The boys'll double up for the night. Bathroom's down the hall. Paul tells me you've got some hanky-panky planned, you naughty man." She floated me a drink on a cardboard coaster.

Ingrid used to kid me and my bachelor ways when I worked with Paul in Toronto and we'd get together for dinners and so on. She made it sound light though I always suspected there was more to it and I believe she was happy to finally convince Paul to make the move to Zurich and away from bad influences, namely me. Besides, she was from Switzerland and always longed to return.

"Jury's still out," I said. "We'll see." I gave her a nudge-nudge-wink-wink type of look and she raised her eyebrows at me. "Hey, Paul, how's your Swiss coming along? I may need a few pointers."

"You'll be fine. It's true, most people do speak English. What happened to you was a fluke. That being said, you're headed to the small towns and what you really need to be aware of is that everyone says 'Gruëzi' to everyone they meet. It's like hello or good day or whatever and if you don't reply in kind you are regarded as some sort of low-life sociopath."

"He's exaggerating."

"It's not an exaggeration. Trust someone who has experienced the stigma of ineptitude." Paul turned to Ingrid. "Remember that young girl who complained to you when I didn't reply to her in the restaurant?"

"She was mentally challenged."

"Beside the point. She was voicing what everyone else felt." Paul swept his arm across the room. "Repeat after me: Gruëzi."

"Gruëzi," I said.

"Close enough. That'll get you through the worst of it. The rest is a cake walk, believe me."

"I still have to buy a ticket to Lenzerheide."

"No problem. I'll be with you. Main thing to remember is you have exactly five minutes to exit the train at Chur, go up the escalator, get to the parking lot and board the bus."

"And if I'm late?"

"Have you seen the Swiss clocks located in all the stations?" Paul asked and I sort of nodded. "When the second hand hits the departure time, the doors close and the bus or the train or whatever departs. You can be chasing behind, loaded down with three suitcases and a child and pet dog in tow, a ticket clenched between your teeth, and it's bye-bye, Charlie!"

"I see. What if the bus is late?"

"The bus is never late."

"Never?"

"Never."

"I think I'm gaining a picture."

"Great," Ingrid said. "Now, tell me, what have you been up to? What brings you here, really? It's been awhile since we've seen you." She topped up the glasses. "I want to know everything."

From the bus station, I rolled my carry-on up the hill to the address given me. The hill was steeper than I thought and I stopped on the flagstones to catch my breath. It was an attractive older house, likely begun as a cabin then rooms added onto and updated over the years with a large sundeck off the second floor and presumably a spectacular view of the surrounding valley, lake and mountains. I rang the doorbell and Sigi answered. She looked fantastic and my gaze was drawn immediately to her one blue and one green eye.

"You made it."

"You sound surprised."

"Shouldn't I be?"

"I said I'd be here."

"Yes, you did. And here you are." She stared at me in a rather quizzical fashion. "Not ... disappointed, I hope?" She rattled the remains of ice in her glass. "I'm having gin and tonic. Would you like one?"

"Love one." I followed her up the stairs to a living room that contained a fireplace surrounded by various couches, tables and chairs plus doors leading to what I presumed to be bedrooms and a bathroom, the kitchen being off to the side. A pair of sliding glass doors opened up to the deck. On the white walls hung numerous nude or semi-nude photographs of Sigi, both in black and white and in colour, most of which were taken, at a guess, when she was in her twenties or early thirties. She handed me a drink and I wandered slowly around the room taking in the photos. Sigi shuffled awkwardly beside me, skipping her feet, bouncing her shoulders, unable to remain still.

"My husband shot most of these. Some are stills from movies or stage productions."

"Uh-huh. They're very good."

"I was younger, of course."

"In Canada it's generally pets and wildflowers on the walls." I studied one of her standing under a waterfall, her nipples poking through a thin fabric. "Do you ever feel … I don't know … uncomfortable? When people come over, I mean? Having these on the walls? Them seeing you like this?"

"You mean nude?" she asked. "Why should I? When you are young, and an actress, you want to be looked at; admired. I had a fairly lovely body, I think. Nothing to be ashamed or embarrassed about."

"You still have a lovely body, in my opinion."

"'In my opinion.' That's very amusing. Why do you see the need to qualify? I wasn't fishing for a compliment, I was stating a fact. And you answer like that. Typical."

"Hmm." I didn't want to piss her off immediately, though it seems I had. I took a breath. "You say your husband shot most of these."

"Yes."

"When you were younger." She saw where I was heading and made a pouty face. "And one day he stopped."

"And one day he stopped, yes. It happens." She crossed her arms and swirled the ice cubes in her glass. "You're laughing. You find that funny?"

"It's not that. I'm just thinking about a line in a poem I read once. It goes: Saying naked reveals itself, we shoot nudes."

"You're saying he enjoyed me as a nude, perhaps not so much naked?"

"Maybe."

"Maybe. And you would enjoy me naked. Maybe."

"Maybe."

"And maybe you will." She leaned in and gave me a kiss on the side of my mouth. "But right now, I'm in the mood for a cigarette. A Gauloise."

"You smoke?"

"Only when I'm in the mood. And then, only Gauloises."

"You have some?"

"No. We have to go to town. Do you mind? We'll go to the Giger bar. Do you know the artist Giger?"

"He designed the monsters in the *Alien* movies, yes?"

"Very good. There's a Giger bar in Chur where all the chairs are shaped like aliens. Shall we go?"

"Sure, why not."

We dropped our glasses and ran hand-in-hand outside to the car, laughing and tittering like a couple of school kids.

"A Mercedes," I said. "Sweet."

"Owning a Mercedes in Switzerland is like owning a Honda in Canada. It's an everyday car."

"Still a Mercedes to me."

"In that case, you drive." She tossed the keys over the roof and we switched sides. "I must warn you though, the sun is going down and there are many hairpin curves along the road. You need to be extremely careful, OK? You may not have noticed this as you rode up on the bus in the daylight."

"I sort of recall it was pretty windy, but I think I can handle it."

"I'm sure you think so. I'll keep you posted anyway."

We eased down the hill and hit the highway. It wasn't so bad. The car handled smoothly and the curves were tight, yeah, but manageable, and I thought I was well settled into the rhythm.

"OK," she announced. "Here comes the first one. Be ready to brake and turn. Most importantly turn."

"Sure," I said, not especially concerned. I cranked the wheel gently and noticed the road ahead had disappeared. I cranked harder and still nothing.

"Harder!" Sigi shouted. "Harder, turn harder! Keep turning!"

I spun the wheel all I was worth and suddenly, instead of the headlights shooting off into space, I could see them mashed against a massive rock face.

"The other way!" Sigi screamed. "Brake, turn, keep turning, keep turning!"

She continued to shout orders and I kept thinking if I turned any harder I'd be staring at my own headlights in the rear view mirror. We broke through the hairpin onto a short straightaway and the two of us burst out in a collective laugh. Whether due to fear, excitement, relief or a combination, I wasn't sure. I do know the adrenaline was definitely flowing.

"We made it," I said.

"Yes, we made it. Only three more to go. And each more dangerous than the first. Like Kafka's guards."

"Yes, except, at the end, we'll be drinking beers and smoking Gauloises among the aliens at the Giger bar. Even Kafka didn't imagine that."

⌒

We were cuddled in the front seat of the car cruising back to the house. It was still only around ten o'clock and Sigi suggested we stop at Nino's Pub for a nightcap. What the hell, I thought. We'd be in bed together soon enough. Besides, we had a full week to look forward to. I pulled the car into a parking lot.

"You're not afraid we'll bump into someone you know?"

"Ah, you mean someone who'll report my indiscretion? Or brand me with the letter 'A' across my chest? Don't worry. While the Swiss people in general may have a reputation as being dour, strict and narrow minded in their own affairs, they are positively libertarian when it comes to the behaviour of their artists. In fact, they expect artists to be wild, crazy, permissive, decadent and even deviant. They'd be disappointed if things were otherwise. Why, the worst thing would be to hide you; keep you to myself. My neighbours would be outraged. They'd feel absolutely snubbed and would hate me for sure. They want to live vicariously through us, why should we prevent them? They see no difference between who we are in life and who we are in our art. It's all to be shared."

"And your husband is good with this?"

"He has his lovers, I have mine. We have an understanding. We make it work."

"I see." We headed into the pub and I tried to remember the word Paul told me. Was it Gratzi? Gertzi? Something like that. Anyway, fuck it. I'm lousy at accents and if anyone says anything close, I'll throw out a *hiya* and see what happens.

We perched on stools at the end of the bar and ordered gin and tonics. I noticed three abandoned drinks across from us, nudged Sigi and motioned with my chin. She grinned and shrugged. There was a pint of green beer, a pint of beer with what appeared to be two scoops of ice cream and a highball glass containing a stir stick, orange slices and a blue liquid that practically glowed in the dark. There was also a round, lipped board holding five dice.

Three guys about my age entered from outside, laughing, bouncing, poking at each other. They leaned against the bar and raised the three glasses. One of the guys laid eyes on Sigi and right away offered some sort of greeting in German. It didn't start with 'G' so I had no idea. Sigi responded and the two of them went on for a minute, then she said "he's from Canada" from which I gathered I was some small part of the conversation. The guy reached out to me for a handshake and gave his name as Max.

"Stanley," I said, lying. I don't know why, maybe

something about what Sigi said in the car, that the locals liked to live vicariously so why not raise the stakes with a certain level of deception?

"Stanley! Stan!" Max said. "Do you know the song 'Stan' by Eminem and Dido?" I shook my head, no. "Check it out. It's pretty good. Not great, but pretty good. You know Eminem? The rapper?"

"Yeah, I've heard of him. I'll be sure to YouTube it when I have the chance."

Having made the polite gesture, Max returned his attentions to Sigi. He was obviously attracted and I could see him trying to make out her eyes in the dim light. "And you are?"

"Stella," she said, without missing a beat.

So that answered the *Streetcar* question, I thought.

"OK, good," Max said. "This is Eric and Conrad. Kurt is out in the cold, smoking."

I pointed at Conrad's beer. "Is that ice cream?"

"Yes. Ice cream. Very good. You try." He shoved the beer at me. "Go on, try!" The other two tilted their glasses in unison. I took a sip. It wasn't half bad. Sigi gave it a try and popped her lips.

"Mm. Different," she said. "What's the green one?"

"Beer with apple schnapps," Max said. We each took a hit.

"And that?" Sigi asked. "It looks positively radioactive."

"Alp Top," Eric, whose English appeared to be the worst, said. He slid the liquid across and we tried it. It was like drinking sweetened furniture remover.

"What's in it?" Sigi made a face and waved a hand in front of her mouth. The guys all laughed uproariously. Eric may have known the ingredients, but he was stuck for the correct English words.

"A girlie drink," Max said. "He's going through the cocktail menu until we get into the hard drinking, later." Max was also stumped as to the ingredients. We called the waitress over.

"Gin, blue curacao, peach liqueur and tonic water," she said. Max waved her closer, whispered in her ear. Next thing you knew she was back with five apple schnapps shooters.

"Prosit!" Max said, and we slammed them back. "You know this game?" He pointed to the dice on the board and Sigi and I shook our heads, no. "It's for gambling and drinking. Very simple."

I figured as much. Turned out these guys grew up together in Lenzerheide, then split after graduation to settle in various parts of Switzerland and Germany. Eric was a veterinarian, married and living in Chur. Conrad was an eco-friendly farmer living outside Stuttgart and engaged to be married in a month. Kurt was a banker in Zurich. Max was a lawyer and recently split and hurting from a five-year steady relationship, clearly intent on finding someone to ease the pain, if only temporarily. He placed the dice in Sigi's hand, gazed into her eyes, gazed deeper, and gave her fingers a squeeze. Apparently, the four amigos plan a ritual meeting one weekend a year in order to catch up, reminisce, bullshit and generally go berserk. This was the weekend. They ended the previous night at four in the morning at Nino's and were back at it again. I noticed a new face had insinuated himself next to Conrad. I assumed it was Kurt. The two said a few words, Kurt shrugged and did a little dance step on his way to the john.

"There are five dice. The object is to roll sixes or ones, the other numbers don't count. A six is worth one point while a one is worth half a point. If you roll two ones, it becomes a six. If you're left with a single one, you have to throw for a six. You can't end with a half point. You keep throwing until your remaining dice are neither a six nor a one. Whoever ends with the least points pays for a round."

I could guess how this would end—as an expensive, four a.m. debauchery at Nino's with a bunch of drunken guys with charge cards nailed to their foreheads, sharing stories of the good old days in sloppy German, maybe singing the old school song, with Max hitting on Sigi every time I turned away—and I wasn't sure I wanted to hang in and watch it play out. Besides, the place was starting to fill up and there'd be plenty of other girls for them to try and impress. Sigi, of course, loved the idea of a game of chance.

"So if I roll and neither a one nor a six come up, I score zero and I pass the dice, yes?" The guys nodded. She rolled the dice across the board and immediately had three sixes. The guys cheered. She rolled again and there was another six. She rolled the final die and another six appeared. She jumped in her seat while the guys whooped amazement. Sigi said something to them in German and they laughed even louder. She turned to me and translated.

"I told them sometimes the dumbest farmer grows the biggest potatoes. It's a saying that means you don't always have to be smart to win, you can be lucky."

The guys all took their turn and Eric placed last. He waved a finger and five more schnapps arrived. Different colour, same result. We banged them back. Sigi clapped her hands and was set to roll again. I grabbed her elbow and pointed to my watch.

"Hey, look at the time, Stella honey! What did we tell the babysitter? Grab your stuff, we gotta get a move on or else it's time and a half." I tossed a twenty franc note on the bar. "Sorry fellas. Nice meeting you. Thanks for the drink. Enjoy your evening."

Sigi opened her mouth to speak and decided to lay a big wet kiss on me instead. "Oh, Stanley, I love it when you're macho!" She blew the guys a kiss. "Have fun! Thanks for teaching me the game." She grabbed her gear and we tumbled onto the street.

Back at the ranch she asked if I didn't mind waiting until morning. To be honest, I was still pretty jet-lagged anyway and nothing worse than trying to have sex when there's the fear of nodding off at the crucial moment. I said, sure, no problem. She waltzed off to the loo. When she stepped out, she proceeded to leave a trail of clothes on the floor behind her. She crawled into bed butt naked beside me, gave me a hug, a kiss, then rolled over on her side. The linens felt clean, fresh and wrinkle free. That wouldn't last.

Next morning we went at each other with a vengeance, up one side and down the other. We agreed it had been a good idea to wait. Sex was followed by a breakfast of coffee, eggs, toast, a variety of fruits, cheeses, sliced meats, champagne and orange juice. Sigi had a tremendous appetite for all of it.

"I can't help myself," she said. "I have a small tank and a lousy metabolism yet I keep stuffing my face. I have to constantly work out to keep down the weight. I ski, I run, I cycle, I hike, go, go, go. Next week I start again. This week, I enjoy."

We went back to bed. I said it would help wear off the calories and she laughed. "If that's the case, I'll be nothing but skin and bones by the end of the week."

Didn't take too many days to realize I'd over packed. The temperature remained in the low to mid-twenties and the two of us wore nothing or next to nothing for the most part of our stay. The fridge and freezer were filled with food. Sigi would pull out steaks and pork tenderloins and elk burgers and wild game sausages and I'd BBQ them outside on the deck. Or else she'd throw together a risotto or polenta and rabbit or rösti with salmon or rösti with meatballs or cheese fondue or raclette or potato dumplings or spätzle with sliced beef. I'd hit the wine cellar and uncork champagne for sex, a nice chablis for fish or a cabernet or rioja for meat. Or mix and match, it didn't matter. Of course, there were always gin and tonics on the go and we spent our time in a constant state of satiated inebriation. The only times we went out were to pick up fresh fruits and vegetables, condoms and maybe the odd pack of Gauloises. We enjoyed smoking on the deck in the evening, bathed in moonlight, gazing across at the stars brightly twinkling atop Forbisch Mountain. It was sublime.

Over a dinner of sauerkraut and sausages I asked if there was a problem with us cleaning out the pantry. No, she said. When Walter came home he'd simply re-stock the supplies. It was something he liked to do: provide for people. Share his good fortune. Perhaps too much so.

"Uh-huh." I considered this, then asked: "You probably get this question a lot. Is he related? Your husband. To Herman Hesse."

"Well, you see, everyone with the last name 'Hess' believes they're somehow related, especially as the population is not large, all things considered. This includes Walter, though he's never actually checked into it. I think he hasn't because he fears disappointment. What do they say: Better a certain probability than an uncertain improbability?"

"Right. Makes some sense. Keep the dream alive and so on. What about kids? Do the two of you have any?"

"No. We were both set on our careers. We neither had the time nor the inclination. Besides, there are enough of us running around the world today. We don't need more gumming up the works."

I stabbed a chunk of sausage with my fork, covered it with sauerkraut and hot mustard and tucked it in my mouth. I chewed slowly and washed it down with a splash of Italian Zinfandel. Sigi walked to the fridge to grab some sparkling water. I picked up my cell and aimed it at her as she returned. She stopped and wagged a finger.

"Don't you dare snap a photo."

We were in our birthday suits, as per usual. "Why not?" I asked. "You look terrific. And I'd like to have a reminder."

"I'll give you a publicity shot of myself. Taken by a professional. I'll even autograph it for you." She mimed her signature in the air.

"It's not the same."

"You'll like it. It doesn't resemble me in the least."

"Please."

"No." She very dramatically stuck her hand out in front of her. "I don't want you to take photos of me here, nude or otherwise. You think I don't read the papers? The last thing I want is a shot of my tits plastered all over Facebook."

"I thought there was no difference, your life and your art. It's all public."

"Don't be a wise guy."

"It's just for me. I wouldn't show anyone." I aimed the cell.

"That's what they all say. Until later, when the bloom is off the rose. No, I told you. You have a picture of me in your head already. That's the best, as it will never fade. A photograph loses its lustre. After a time, it's nothing but cheap nostalgia at best, at worst, pornography."

"What about your movies, where you're naked?"

"In the movies, I'm not naked, I'm nude. They paid me. There's the difference. Here, with you, I'm naked. It's between us. What was that line of poetry you quoted me? Saying naked reveals itself, we shoot nudes, yes? I'm inclined to believe that. Do you remember who wrote it?"

"No. I think I was browsing through a used bookstore, flipping pages. I spotted it. The line struck me. That's all I remember of the poem."

"You see, it's the same with us. We'll remember the best parts. For me, I have a tiny reel of film of us in my head that I'll be able to replay whenever I want." Sigi pressed a finger to her temple. "You'll be disappointed to know it doesn't consist entirely of your cock, though you do have a handsome cock. There are other images. The way you close your eyes when you take a first bite of food, as if relishing the moment. The way you describe a situation using your hands—very funny. Your nose."

"My nose?"

"Yes, your nose. You have a regal nose. It commands respect." She smiled. "And, of course, the first time you reached your hands under my ass and raised me off the bed to drive deeper. It made me gasp. Things like that."

She put on her bathrobe, walked out to the deck, gripped the rail and stared out at the night. A pale moon hung above Forbisch Mountain. Sigi lit a Gauloise. I slipped into my own bathrobe and followed her. She was softly crooning an old standard.

"It's only a paper moon, sailing over a cardboard sea, but it wouldn't be make believe ... da-da, da-da, da-dee ..."

Her voice trailed. I reached around, under her robe and gently squeezed her breasts, played with her nipples. "You know," she said, "I've never made love outdoors. Can you believe that? A woman my age." I crept my fingers down between her legs. She was sopping wet. I grew hard instantly. I opened my bathrobe, raised hers and pressed my body in tight. She pushed up on her toes and bent over the railing. I inched slowly inside her. She took a deep drag on the Gauloise and shuddered.

It was our final night together.

～

Next morning, I awoke and could hear Sigi getting breakfast on in the kitchen. I crawled from bed, hit the shower, got dressed. I walked to the living room and took a quick peek at the walls. All the previous photos of her were gone, replaced by family portraits of her and her husband along with a couple of kids at various ages. She wandered over, rested her chin on a fist, and studied them with me.

"What's this?" I asked.

"This is reality."

"Your kids."

"Yes."

"Where are they?"

"They're not kids anymore, if that's what you think. They're adults, out in the world, living their own lives."

"Why ...?" The word floated out of my mouth, into the air, somehow disconnected from anything.

"I wanted to fulfill a young man's fantasy: an affair

with an older woman—an aging movie star—in an exotic location. I didn't want to spoil it with reminders of childbirth and stretch marks and milk-filled breasts once used as feeding bags for colic-y, snotty-nosed babies. So, I sweetened the scene with perfectly lit, perfectly shot, 8x10 glossies from a more idyllic era."

"I see."

"You see. Good! Now, it's over—*poof!* We had our fun. I begin rehearsals in Zurich, my husband returns from Brazil, you return to Toronto. Nice while it lasted. Thank you very much for the swell time."

"We can keep in touch."

"I think not. I'll drop you off at the bus station with a polite kiss on the cheek, after that ..." She snapped her fingers. "C'est tout." She stroked my nose with her hand, spun on her heels and retreated to the kitchen. I stood there, alone among a frozen array of innocent, blissful, smiling faces.

I ordered a gin and tonic on the plane. Naturally, I had known all along that Sigi had kids as I'd Googled her those several months ago, wanting to know more about her. It was also no secret she and her husband were splitting and having to sell their home sweet home due to him having an affair with another, much younger, woman. Gossip travels at warp speed in the entertainment industry. I was made aware before I left Toronto and apprised again by Paul and Ingrid in Zurich. And

Sigi was no dummy—she knew that I knew, it goes without saying. It didn't matter. The situation was all so banal, so tawdry, the most we could do was play our designated roles to the best of our abilities and attempt to transform the mundane into something that resembled art. Perhaps not high art, but art nonetheless.

I appreciated Sigi making the effort to create a dream that included me. She was correct on one level. There was a small reel of film in my head containing many beautiful memories which I could replay anytime I wanted: our fear-filled drive down the mountain, smoking Gauloises at the Giger Bar, her standing naked in the doorway, one green eye and one blue eye. Though I knew even this piece of film couldn't last forever. Nothing does.

And so it goes.

Whether it's the staged image of some poor sap stood in the pouring rain under a second floor window hollering "Stella" at the top of his lungs, or a similar heartbroken soul leaned against a moonlit balcony rail, humming: "It's only a paper moon, sailing over a cardboard sea, but it wouldn't be make believe ...," it's the same. There occurs the sobering recognition that whatever part we play, and however well we play it, the performance (as well as the particular details) fades and disappears soon after the curtain falls.

And so it goes.

And so it goes.

THE MARRIAGE COUNSEL'S TALE

*In which a young couple attempts to save their
marriage by seeking advice from a home audience
via a do-it-yourself internet program.*

The two fuss at the foot of the basement stairs leading
into the den. They face a slim full-length mirror,
Maddie in front, Jonathan tight behind her, making last
minute adjustments to their wardrobes. Jonathan zips
the back of her dress and latches her necklace. Maddie
checks her lipstick and hair in a compact. She licks and
rubs lipstick from her teeth. They bicker jokingly.

Maddie, that is just so not true. It is true, Jonathan.
Is not. Is. Maddie, honey, I never said that. Johnny, sweetie, you did. I'm sure I didn't. I'm sure you did. Why
would I say that? Exactly. Why. Because I didn't, that's
why. But you did. You did. I don't believe it. I'm telling
you. I didn't. You did. Honey ... Sweetie ... sweetie ... you
did, you did, you really did ... OK, OK, I give up. Have it
your way.

He pulls at his face and smells his breath in a cupped
hand.

Maddie, Maddie, Maddie. Darling. What the hell are
we doing? I mean, really? We both thought it would be
a good idea. Remember? I seem to recall it was more

your idea. You said it was worth a try. Yeah, well, I think I've changed my mind. Haha. A bit late for that. You're not having second thoughts? You wouldn't agree to see a marriage counsellor. C'mon love. What do I keep saying? We don't need a marriage counsellor. We can work things out on our own. Other people do. A little give and take, that's all. Uh-huh.

Maddie adjusts the position of her breasts by tugging at her dress straps.

Besides, marriage counsellors are as screwed up as the next guy, maybe more so.

Oh, and you know this because ...? It just makes sense. Anyone who'd want a job listening to couples bitch and complain all day long has to be a bit ... you know ...

Jonathan twirls a finger around his ear.

It's not normal. Johnny, honey, we need to involve a third party; someone outside the situation; someone without a vested interest; someone neutral. The situation? Baby, what situation? We're going through a rough patch, that's all. It happens to everyone. We're no different. It'll pass.

Maddie bends into the mirror and pops her painted lips.

If we ignore it. I didn't say that. You didn't have to. It's your way. My "way"? Jonathan uses his fingers as quotes.

What the hell does that mean? My "way"? The knocking sound in the car, says Maddie. Oh, c'mon. The leak in the bathroom. Totally different issues altogether. Your brother, when he told you ... OK, OK ... and you let it go ... OK, yes, you're right. ... until it was too late ... All right, all right. You win. I dropped the ball on that one. I admit it. Jeez. Gimme a break. You'd think someone died or something. Besides, what was I supposed to do? Exactly. You see? Excuses. We need to talk. Oh, you mean you need to talk. All right, I need to talk. But that's part of the problem, isn't it? You refuse to talk about anything. Oh, c'mon, that's not fair. I talk about things. Not the important things.

Maddie straightens. The two speak to each other eye to eye in the mirror.

Honey, I do. Sweetie, you don't. Baby, I do. You don't. I do. Johnny, you don't. You never do. Maddie, you're wrong, I absolutely do. I'm telling you, sweetie, you don't. You never talk. OK, can we drop this? Can we? Please?

Jonathan straightens his tie, strikes a pose and flashes his pearly whites.

How do I look?

Maddie twists her mouth, makes with the hard glare.

You see, sweetie pie? You refuse to talk.

She spins, gives his hair a swipe, spins back to pull at her own hair.

You look fine; terrific. I feel like a monkey in a freaking circus about to perform. How did you find out about this pod-cast thing in the first place? Vicki. Vicki? Figures. You don't like Vicki. Not that I don't like her. A bit too New Age, airy-fairy, Dr. Phil, for me. That's all. Oho, and when did you ever watch Dr. Phil? Don't need to, darling. Baby, you wouldn't know Dr. Phil if he shit in your shoe. Haha. Right. Pretty weird though, a reality show that feeds from a camera in the comfort of your own home. How does that work? Magic.

Maddie's eyes widen and she throws her hands in the air. She goes back to her compact and lipstick.

I'm serious. So am I. I really don't know. I called a number. Someone came over, set up the equipment, gave me instructions, left. They make a lot of money with this? Jonathan, I don't know; I don't care. It's a fair question. All I know is there's a waiting list of people who want to be on the show and—according to Vicki—we were damn lucky to be chosen. Yeah, I bet there's a waiting list. Crazy people everywhere dying to be on camera. Jonathan; sweetie.

She drops her arms to her sides and visibly sags. Jonathan places his hands on her waist and kisses the top of her head.

Sorry, honey. You checked out the program? Due diligence and all that? Once. And? It was fine. No great shakes. I mean, it's like TV, only, on computer. What do you expect? Anyway, it's a start. Fine. Fine. Anyway, I don't refuse to talk, baby, I refuse to argue. There's a big difference. Christ, I'm getting a headache already and we haven't even started. You're overreacting. I'm not overreacting. A headache. Here. Between the eyes. Do you want an aspirin?

She fishes in her purse. Jonathan squints a baby face.

Aspirin upsets my stomach.

Maddie snaps the purse shut and stamps a foot.

It's always the same. Anytime I want to talk, you get a headache. That's not true. It is. It isn't. Honey, it is. Sweetie, it isn't. It is. Every single time. Honey, that's just not true. It is so true. Every time I want to talk. Baby ...

You get a goddamn headache. Ohhhhh! Fine, fine. Here we go. Fine. Let's go hang out our dirty laundry in front of a bunch of total strangers. Fine. Why not?

Maddie takes a breath and releases a long sigh.

Johnny, I wish you wouldn't be this way. Can't you look at this more as a forum for discussion? Something positive?

She relaxes, pokes at the air with her lipstick; speaks as if reciting from an article she's read.

Studies have shown that it's good to get things out in the open and that, in fact, it's easier to talk in front of strangers about personal problems than to people you know or love since you feel less judged by them. There's hard data. And, in this case, the strangers aren't even here—they're out in la-la land somewhere. All we have to do is talk. There'll be some kind of survey at the end, that's it. Besides, it might be fun. We might learn something about each other that we didn't know before.

Jonathan brushes invisible dandruff from his dress jacket. He almost whispers.

Yeah, that's what I'm afraid of. What does that mean? Nothing, darling. No, sweetie, I'm curious. What? Nothing. Uh-huh? Oh, it just means there's probably enough to deal with already—stuff we already know—without bringing up something new. That's all. Hmm. I see. What's the time?

Jonathan checks his watch.

Almost. I could use a drink right now. Uh-huh. I could use a cigarette. You should think about quitting. Seriously. Look who's talking.

She pokes his belly with a finger.

You're getting a beer belly. Too many liquid lunches and not enough exercise. Hey, don't you recognize love handles when you see them? Oh, that's what you call them, huh?

She tickles him, reaches around behind, grabs his ass and feigns a bit of sex, doggie-style.

And you don't use a tack hammer to drive a spike, is that how it works? Uh-uh-uh ... Haha. Nice try, buster. OK, OK, cut it out already.

Jonathan pushes away, turns his back to Maddie, hikes his dress jacket and tries to check himself out in the mirror.

You think my ass is getting big? I'm joking. Your ass is fine. It's perfect. Perfect? Perfect. You look very handsome. Thank you for doing this. It means a lot to me. It does. Umm. You don't find the whole thing slightly embarrassing; a bit pathetic, even? I mean ... I think it's important. For both of us. Really. OK. I suppose.

She nuzzles his neck with her nose and slips her feet into a pair of black pumps. C'mon. Cheer up.

She crosses the floor to the couch and sits. She motions Jonathan to join her. He straightens his jacket.

I'm glad one of us is enjoying this. Oh ... what the hell. Let's knock 'em dead. Thank Christ this program's only local.

He picks up the remote on the way and checks out the equipment. Maddie plays with the hem of her dress.

It is only on local, right? That's what you told me? Low budget.

Maddie smiles, shrugs, bounces on her toes. Jonathan moans; sits.

Great. Just great. Is it time? Yeah, it's time. We're on.

Jonathan hits the remote. The theme song kicks in:
Love Is Strange. The song fades. The two stare at the mon-
itor for a moment, unsure as to how to begin. They look
around awkwardly. Maddie glares at Jonathan.

Well?

Jonathan waves the remote at the screen.

I thought there might be a host of some sort. On the
screen. I already told you there wouldn't be. Not a 'host'
exactly; a voice-over or something; an introduction. No.
I wrote everything out for you. Didn't you read it? I
looked at it. You looked at it? Do you still have it? Yeah,
yeah, I still have it. Right here.

He snaps open a folded piece of paper from his breast
pocket, grins and speaks toward the camera.

Sorry about that. It wasn't made clear to me I thought
it was pretty clear. I found it clear. I found it a bit con-
fusing, myself. I found it very clear. What part was con-
fusing to you, sweetie? Doesn't matter, honey. I've got
it now. If you were confused, darling, why didn't you
ask? I've got it. Look—here it is. There's an opening
blurb, yes? Written? Yes, there's an opening blurb. I just
wasn't sure ... that's all. Under control now. We're on ...
y'know? I know we're on. I know. Um, hi and welcome
to the new reality program, *Love Is Strange*, the show
where couples going through crisis come together to
share their thoughts, ideas and 'feelings' to an internet
audience.

He re-folds the paper and taps it against his knee. He glances at Maddie.

Y'know, darling, I wouldn't say we're going through a "crisis", exactly. No, sweetie? Not exactly. Not yet. Not yet? OK, right, so ... OK, we might as well begin. Umm ...

He rubs his forehead with the palm of his hand, the hand holding the paper.

Oh, crap. What is it now? I'm trying to remember the order. I wrote it down for you. It's all there. No need to shout at me. Honey. I'm not shouting. Sweetie. I'm simply saying. You don't have to remember it. You can read it. It's introductions first, yes? Where we each introduce ourselves. I know it's introductions first. That makes sense. I'm not a complete idiot. I never said you were. No? No. I wasn't sure, that's all. I see. Do you? Not really. Uh-huh. Did you want to do the honours?

He makes a sweeping gesture with the paper and dangles it in front of Maddie. The pair catch each other peripherally, keeping their main focus on the camera.

You go ahead. You're sure? Yes. OK. Sure. Sure, I can start. No problem. It's only the introduction. No, that's fine, love. I'll start. Hi everyone.

Jonathan stops and laughs. He half-turns to Maddie.

I feel like I'm supposed to say: Hi. My name is Jonathan and I'm an alcoholic. If the shoe fits ... Haha, very funny. You're the one who said it. Let's forget it, OK? OK? OK. Hi, my name is Jonathan Edwards ...

Maddie lets out a snort.

Right. What? Your name is Jonathan Edwards. Yeah, so? All I'm saying. All you're saying is what? That ... your name ... My name? Wasn't ... always ... Wasn't always what? Jonathan Edwards. Are you kidding me? All I'm saying. That was my dad's doing, not mine. He made the change. I had nothing to do with it. You went along with it. I was a kid. A goddamn kid. I had no say in the matter. None. You could've changed it back. You had no problem changing your name when we got married. That was then. Things are different now. Oh, that's right. Maddie's re-discovering her roots; her Greek heritage. She thinks she's descended from royalty or something; or, no, a long line of goddesses. Isn't that right, darling? No need to get nasty, cupcake. Who's getting nasty here? The first words out of my mouth and you're already at me. Lots of people change their names and for different reasons. My dad was trying to start a new business in a new country and he figured Dmitrios Anagnostopoulos was just too much of a mouthful. It's that simple. I don't know why you want to make such a big deal out of it. It's just a name. A rose is a rose is a rose ... Is that it? Shall I go on, or what?

Maddie shrugs. Jonathan clicks his tongue and gives his neck a crack.

OK. I'm thirty-two years old, my family's in the sea-food industry ... They're fishermen. Fine, they're fishermen. Nothing wrong with that. Never said there was. Just wanting to be clear. Uh-huh. My dad also has a seafood shop in Kensington Market. Small, but it brings in a buck or two. As for me, I own and operate a company called Minotaur Investments ... Which belonged to my father and which I brought Jonathan into ... and which eventually I took over and turned into a success after your father almost drove it into the ground. He was old, he couldn't keep up. Be that as it may ... Fine. I'll give the devil his due ... Thank you. Thank you very much. I don't see you suffering. What else? What else? That's it. Us? Oh yeah. Of course. Goes without saying. Maddie and I have been together for ... what? ... nine years and married for three of those nine. Correct? OK, love, your turn.

Jonathan leans back in the couch and stretches his arms along the back. Maddie composes herself by drumming her fingers on her closed knees.

Thank you. My name is Maddie ... umm, Madeleine Edwards, née Kronos. I'm thirty-four years old and I formerly helped manage my father's company until he retired and Jonathan took over the reins. At that point, Jonathan decided it didn't befit his position as the new president to have me working, and so, I was relegated to the position of "wife" of the president of Minotaur Investments ... Wait a minute, wait a minute! Whoa! We talked about this.

Jonathan insinuates himself forward and fidgets his clasped hands across his thighs. He taps his thumbs together.

We did. You said you were bored; you wanted to try something different; something that better suited you and your interests; your ... talents ... Umm. That's true. He's right. I was bored. The business had changed; had grown larger; become less personal and more dependent on technology. Computers and so on. Lawyers. Bankers. And accountants. My God, accountants.

They both laugh in agreement at this. Jonathan rolls back and stretches out.

I was not even vaguely interested on any level. Jonathan, however, leapt in with both feet until there was less and less for me to do. Hey—why work if you don't have to? Am I right? Or am I wrong? Sweetheart? Darling ... you think playing "hostess" to a bunch of shallow, idiotic, two-faced stuffed shirts and their Stepford Wives isn't work? Honey, they're not that bad. They're not. Be nice, smile, serve some drinks, a few canapés—they're happy. How hard can it be? Totally boring, self-centred and without any redeeming qualities. Bottom feeders. There are worse things. True. As I was to find out ... Maddie, sweetheart ... don't. Fine. I won't. What's next on the list, honey?

Jonathan snaps the paper open, shrugs towards the camera and reads.

Well, darling, it's hobbies. Seems safe enough. I don't have a lot of time for hobbies, really, though I like to watch some sports on TV. Football, baseball, mainly. I played ball when I was younger In fact, I almost made Triple A as a shortstop, except, I had a trick knee. Oh, don't be so modest Jonathan ... you're still a bit of a ball player, aren't you? Trick knee or not. I mean, you like to toss the old pigskin around now and again. Yeah, I guess. When I have the time. With a few of the guys. What about you, Maddie? Any hobbies?

Maddie smiles and grows animated with the topic.

I enjoy gardening. I'm very into growing my own vegetables and herbs. I'm also going through an intense period of self-discovery and re-evaluation at the present moment; taking classes, keeping a personal journal, jotting down ideas, dreams; writing small poems, songs, that sort of thing. Uh-huh. And she's also learning to read auras. People's auras.

He gives his hands a fingers a vague shake.

With Vicki, right honey?

He glances at Maddie to see if she's going to say something. She doesn't. He purses his lips, like: whatever, and nods.

Cool. OK, next item is: What is the most positive aspect of our relationship? Umm. OK, I would say, the life we've built together. You mean: lifestyle, sweetie. Whatever. You? The sex.

Jonathan is caught by surprise.

In the beginning. Lately, so-so. Work has been crazy these days. You wouldn't believe ... No excuses. Next item. Least positive aspect.

Jonathan makes a weak attempt at a joke.

Notice how nobody wants to say the word "negative" anymore? "Least positive". Gimme a break. Ha! Yeah, that's hilarious. OK, OK. Least positive? The fact that Maddie doesn't understand the pressures I'm under and doesn't appreciate the amount of time and work that's necessary to run a successful business these days. That's two aspects. They tie together. Your turn. Least positive, I guess—and there are several—is that, while you have plenty of time for your business, you have no time for me; for us.

Jonathan leans and turns his full attention to the camera. In fact, they try to outdo each other for the spotlight.

I have time for you. You don't. I do. You don't. Sweetie, I do. No, honey, you don't. Yes, I do. No, you don't. That's not fair. I do. You do not. You have no time. I have time. I do. You never have time. Never. You're always busy. Baby ... No, sweetie, you never do. OK, OK. Always need the last word. And what time you do have, you prefer to share with other women.

Jonathan drops his jaw and wraps his hands behind his head. Maddie's hands flutter the air.

Christ. C'mon ... we've been through this. Do you deny it? Once. One time. I admitted it then, I admit it now. In front of witnesses. It was a weak moment. It was a mistake. Too much to drink. I apologized. I'm only human. I'm sorry. It won't happen again. What more do you want from me? Once? One time? One woman?

She stares at Jonathan who stares back and offers a resolute nod. He crosses his heart with his thumb. She shrugs.

OK. Next item.

Maddie smiles. Jonathan bobs his head up and down and reads.

What do you want from this relationship? OK, more than anything—support. I want Maddie's support. I want her there behind me. Behind you? With me. OK? With me.

His cell phone rings.

Jonathan? You're not going to answer that. Sorry. I thought I had it turned off. Sorry.

He checks the number on the screen, turns the phone off and tucks it away.

Um, the business is growing. It has a chance to really take off. We can both benefit if we focus. It means the opportunity to make a lot of money and a chance to move up in the world; really move up: new house, new cars, travel ... Sounds great. Sounds fantastic. Yeah. Yeah, it does. And what do you want, Maddie? Huh? What is it you want? Children. I want children, Jonathan. Your children. I'm tired of the business. Take the business. I'm not getting any younger. Call it stereotypical, call it biological clock, I don't care. I want children. Children? That's a big step. Children. Wow! I didn't know. I never suspected. I thought ... I mean, I'm not against having children. I'm not. I'm just not so sure it's the right time. Another two or three years, I figure, and yeah, maybe. When we're really established; when the money's there.

They argue their cases to the television audience.

We have the money; money is not the problem. The problem is you. I think ... I feel, that, you don't want to be married to a "mother"; you don't want to be seen by people ... certain people ... as a "father". It would cramp your style. That's crazy. Where do you get an idea like that? I told you, I feel it ... I sense it. Oh, here we go. Another thing to put under the "least positive" list. The whole aura reading thing. And ... she's found God. Only, not the God that most people find. No, she's created her own, a sort of mix and match; the best of east meets west; she's on some kind of pseudo-religious kick. She's into homeopathic remedies and healing hands and past lives and spirit guides and ESP and Tarot card reading and herbal medications and out-of-body experience and witchcraft and ... and ... what else? Huh? What other bogus voodoo? I don't know; I can't keep up. So now she figures she can read minds and pick up on vibrations and channel energy fields and whatnot.

Maddie's face tenses, her tone gets serious.

Don't mock what you don't understand. Honey, I'm just saying ... Don't. Please. It's just ... It doesn't matter. Really. It's my journey. I'm not asking you to agree with it, sweetie. I'm not. Though I would appreciate it if you took it somewhat seriously.

Jonathan takes a second and grits his teeth.

You're right. I'm sorry. Baby, I'm sorry. I'm trying, I really am. It's just that, sometimes, it seems ... too much, y'know? I don't get it. I can't wrap my head around it. I feel totally out of place. I understand. I do. And it's OK. It's not easy stuff, I know. It's not easy for me sometimes, either. I just wish you'd try a little harder, love, that's all.

Jonathan smiles and touches her hand with his own.

OK. Shall I go on? OK. The final item on the list is: Choose a song from the Karaoke menu that best describes your relationship.

He fumbles with the remote. Maddie leans in.

You just press the number of the song. The words appear on the screen and the music comes out through the speakers. Right. Got it. Here's what I picked. I normally have a few drinks before I do this sort of thing, haha. All right, here goes.

He stands, presses buttons on the remote and uses it as a microphone. He clears his throat and smiles at the audience. He sings and dances to Barry White's *My First, My Last, My Everything*.

> ... I know there's only one like you
> There's no way they could have made two
> Girl you're my reality
> But I'm lost in a dream
> You're my first, my last, my everything ...

Jonathan performs a small bow. He's worked himself into a bit of a lather and he's puffing slightly. Maddie grins and applauds ecstatically.

Oh, Jonathan, that was so sweet. That was the song that was playing on the radio the night you proposed to me. I can't believe you remembered that. Well, there you go. And long ... it's a long song. Yeah, it is long, isn't it? Yeah, really long. Wow. I didn't realize at the time. And you even had it memorized. I'm impressed. I tried. I mean, I had to cheat a bit, and I flubbed a few lines ... And the dancing ... Very sexy. Yeah, I still got a few moves ... Maybe could've used a lesson or two, but ... No, you were great. Really, really great. Terrific.

She grabs his hand, drags him close and kisses him on the mouth.

Thank you. It was beautiful. Yeah, yeah. Thank you. OK. Whew! So ... what song did you pick, love?

Maddie reaches behind the couch, pulls out a guitar and ducks her head through the strap.

What's this? Well, I didn't think any of the songs they offered were quite suitable, so I wrote my own. You wrote your own? What do you mean, you wrote your own? Christ, Maddie, what the hell? Now, you see ... this is what I'm talking about—you can't just follow instructions, you have to go and change things to suit yourself. I don't believe it. This is just embarrassing. I mean, I didn't even know you could play guitar. Can you play guitar? It's been years, but I've been practicing up. I don't believe it. This is unbelievable. The instructions clearly say pick a song from the list. There're over five hundred goddamn songs on the list and you couldn't find one? I don't believe it. Do you want to hear it or not?

She stands with her guitar at the ready. Jonathan sits.

Sure. Sure. What the hell? It's your moment. Over five hundred goddamn songs. I don't believe it. Then again, I do. Makes perfect sense. Jonathan? Johnny? Please. I'm sorry. I'm sorry. Go ahead, make me look like a jerk. Play. I can't ... I can't play, if you're going to be like that. What do you want me to say? I'm not trying to make you look like a jerk. I'm not. The song you chose was wonderful and sweet and loving and ... and you were fantastic. You really were.

She appeals to the home audience, claps, kisses Jonathan on the cheek.

Wasn't he fantastic? You were. And I'm sorry if you think I've changed the rules, it's just that ... it's important for me, right now, to sing my song rather than someone else's. Y'see? OK. OK. So, let's hear it.

Johnny's just a boy, his head is full of dreams.
He likes singing songs and whatever life brings.
Gonna travel 'round the world and learn a few things
And then he'll build something really big.

Maddie is a girl with romantic notions.
She stands in the rain 'cause she misses the ocean.
And she works real hard to cover emotion
But she wouldn't mind being kissed.

Now they're meant for each other it's easy to see
'cause Maddie can't seem to find her own philosophy
and Johnny's most alive when he's got his head
     between her knees
but in the back of their minds they're saying
... OOOHH THIS IS FUCKED ...
... OOOHH THIS IS FUCKED ...
... OOOHH ...

And now Maddie and Johnny are doomed from the
     start
'cause each one's trying to follow their heart.
And when they're together they're really apart.
It's not the way they said it would be.

Now he's drinking lots of beer 'cause he don't need
    the strife.
She's adding spice to her food to make up for her life.
And each one secretly carries a knife.
This crazy little thing called love.
Oh yeah.

Maddie returns the guitar behind the couch. She cozies
up to Jonathan who sits speechless.

Wow ... That was ... fantastic. Totally fantastic. A bit
scary, maybe, but, fantastic. And this is how you feel ...
really ... about the two of us? About our marriage? I
mean, the whole knife thing, and all? That's pretty
scary. Jonathan, don't be so literal. I only mean ... I feel
we're drifting apart and no amount of money is going
to fix that. And you really want to have a baby? You
think that will make a difference? You think we're
ready? I'm ready. Shall we ask the audience and see what
they have to say?

Both stand and face the audience. They take each
other's hands.

What do you think? Should we have a baby? All those
in favour?

The screen lights up with one huge, increasing number. Maddie bounces on the couch cushions and tugs at
Jonathan's jacket.

Wow! Look at that!

The theme music rises and fades. The couple waves
to the camera as the screen turns blue. Jonathan flips

Maddie onto her back. He slips his hands under her dress.

I'm not wearing underwear, Maddie says.

Jonathan rears back and loosens his tie.

Pretty sure of yourself, yes?

Pretty sure. Yes.

Maddie lifts her hips and pulls the remote out from under. She points the thing at the TV screen and hits a button. The screen turns black. Jonathan unzips his pants.

Come to daddy, he says.

Come to mommy, she replies.

THE NEWLYWEDS' TALE

*In which past events serve to not only destroy
a marriage but also inflict revenge upon a
family beyond any reasonable limits.*

The snow-covered prairie unrolls like a vast sheet of corrugated cardboard, gently rising and falling beyond the blurred horizon. The snow is fresh. There is little to interrupt the whiteness: bent backs of wheat stalks poking through, thin line of fence posts, lone shadow of a circling hawk. A black gash of newly ploughed gravel road pointing north bisects the scene into equal halves. There's a low stand of trees to the east crowned with snow. Off the main road a narrower ploughed artery bleeds east to west as far as a farmhouse. Otherwise there is merely the stamp of boot paths leading around the house to the barn, the shed, the woodpile and so on: evidence of daily chores occurring despite the weather, the worst now over. The sky has cleared and it's an almost windless afternoon with smoke rising straight up from the chimney.

Inside, a man jostles burning wood with a metal poker and adds a fresh log to the pile. He uses the flared end of a dried stick to re-light his pipe, shakes off the flame, tosses the stick on the hearth, eases himself backward into a sofa chair. He crosses one knee with an ankle and smokes. A golden lab lies at one side of the chair. The two stare into the fireplace. A voice issues from the kitchen followed by a woman wearing an apron. She rubs her hands with a dishtowel.

"Should be back soon."

"Yeah."

The woman steps behind the chair and rubs her hands as if trying to remove something other than water. "Nice fire you got going."

"Yeah, I figured."

"Uh-huh."

"Kinda nice. Weather and so on."

"Umm."

The two remain quiet. The woman wipes her nose with the towel. The man chews the stem of his pipe. The two of them sigh.

"She's pretty excited."

"Sure. Not everyday you get married."

"I can't believe it. A week today. Our little girl."

"Not so little."

"Maybe."

The man taps ashes into the ashtray and sets the pipe down. He drags a hand through his thin hair and pulls at his stubbled chin.

"What do you think?" the woman asks.

"What do I think? About what?" There's no verbal response from the woman though the man can sense her reaction, a habit she has, chewing the inside of her lower lip as she waits out a reply. He gives in with a slight shrug of shoulders. "Don't know. Hope for the best, I guess."

"Yeah. She loves him. I know that much."

"Umm. Is it enough, is what I'm wondering."

"You don't think he loves her?"

"I don't know. Seems to. Can't say he doesn't. It's just ..."

"Yeah."

"Funny. Him being gone almost a dozen years, shows up out of the blue, snap, just like that, not here more'n a few weeks, settles in, gets a job, next thing he's courting our Jenny. Why?"

"I know. Funny."

"After what happened."

"It was a long time ago."

"Time heals all wounds, that it?"

"Maybe. People change."

"I hope."

"Anyway, it's not up to us, it's up to Jenny."

"Jenny, yeah. Though more Warren, I think. She'd've waited, seems to me. Taken more time. Instead."

"Less than six months. Getting married Saturday."

"Seems too fast."

"How long for us? Not much different, I think."

"Difference is we were older. Older when we met, older when we married, older when we had her. Old enough to know our own minds."

"Jenny knows. In her heart she knows. Where it counts."

"I still say."

"Nothing you can say. Nothing either of us can say. It's done."

"Uh-huh. In her heart. OK. I'll keep my fingers crossed. Thinking back, though. That look he gave me when they took him away."

"He was a boy."

"That's what scares me. He was a boy. That a boy could give such a look. Filled with such hatred."

"Maybe you've exaggerated. Maybe you've allowed it to grow inside your head all out of proportion."

"You think?"

"I'm just sayin'."

"Maybe. Maybe." He slumps into the chair and stares off into the flames. His arm drops and he mechanically scratches the dog's ears. The woman gives the dishtowel a shake and returns to the kitchen.

~

The two of them are in the local diner finishing off hamburger dinners. Their conversation is animated with youthful energy, nervous bounce and rapid gesticulations. They wave arms, bob heads, lean in and out, grab at hands, squeeze, kiss, release. They laugh out loud, roar, whisper. They push aside plates and drink Cokes. The boy wraps his fingers around the girl's wrists. He looks straight in her eyes. His tone grows serious.

"Jenny," he says.

"What? What is it?"

"I have terrific news."

"You found us a place?" She smiles and rubs his fingertips with hers.

"Sort of. Not exactly. Better."

"Better? What better?"

"I didn't tell you, but I've been lookin' for a different position."

"You mean your job? I thought you loved workin' at the hardware store?"

"Not a different job, a different position. Management."

"Uh-huh?"

"And I got one. With a major chain."

"Yeah?"

"Yeah. Thing is … it's in Toronto."

The girl relaxes her grip, her body sags. "Toronto?"

"Yeah, isn't that great? We'll be able to get outta this dump and live in the city. What d'ya think? Terrific, right?"

"Um … I don't know."

"You don't know? I thought you'd be excited."

"I'm sorry … I just thought … I assumed … we'd be stayin' here."

"Stay here? Why? For what? There's nothin' for us here. It's a shit hole. I'm sorry but it's true. The place is dead. It's practically a ghost town. Everyone's movin' out. All the young people anyhow. If I stay here any longer I'll go crazy. We'll both go crazy. I'm tellin' you."

"I didn't know that. I thought you liked it here."

"Are you kiddin'? What's to like? I hate it. Nothin' but wheat fields for miles. Dust in the summer and mud in the winter. Everyone workin' two or three jobs to make ends meet. Or else on some kind of social assistance or welfare. I wanna make a life for us. A better life. I can't do it here."

"Why'd you come back then? In the first place?"

"Don't know. Thought I had to. Maybe prove somethin' t'myself. Everyone else."

"Prove what?"

"That I'm OK. That I'm not a fuck-up. Back then, I was taken away and stuck in a home. This time, I'm leavin' on my own terms. My choice. Y'understand? The difference?"

"Yeah, I guess. Only, what am I gonna do in the city? Out here, I've got my parents. I've got my horse. I've a got a job."

"There's horses near Toronto if you wanna ride. And your job? I mean, c'mon, gimme a break, I don't wanna knock it, but you sell tickets and popcorn at the theatre, what's that? You can do that anywhere. Besides, theatre's gonna go belly up any day now. As for your parents, we're gonna be married, right? Husband and wife. We wanna have a house and kids and a dog and maybe a cat, yeah? Give them a good life, right?" He strokes her arms and smiles. "Right?"

"What about Saskatoon? Did you like it there? It's pretty big. Maybe we could live there awhile, y'know, get used to things?"

"I don't wanna talk about Saskatoon, OK? I've got nothin' good to say about that place either. It was a prison to me. I just wanna forget about it and everythin' that happened there, clear?"

"Yeah, clear. It just seems like so much so soon."

"What do we wanna wait for? You love me, yes?" She nods. "And I love you. That's what matters. That's what's important. So let's go for it. I'm tellin' you. Toronto! Nice shops, nice restaurants, things to see, things to do ... You're gonna love it. I promise."

"When?"

"They want me to start March First. Plenty of time to get things organized here, make our good-byes and so on. 'Course, I gotta be there a bit sooner to get the lay o' the land, find us a place, figure out what's what, y'know?"

"Sure, makes sense. You really want this, yeah?"

"What's not to want? We get to Toronto, it's a quick flight to New York, Boston, Chicago ... the world! Wherever we want. Think about it."

"OK," she says quietly. He jiggles her hands and her face lights up. "OK."

"OK. That's my girl. Let's pay the bill and go back to my apartment, huh? We'll have some fun. Celebrate."

⌁

The two are naked in bed. On the side table a wadded Kleenex hides a used condom. Jenny has the sheet pulled over her breasts while Warren lies totally exposed, his penis damp and limp between his legs. He has an arm wrapped around her shoulders and runs his fingertips up and down her neck. She's in a half-turn and pulls gently at the hairs on his chest.

"How many kids ya want?" he asks.

"Don't know, haven't given it much thought. Two, anyway."

"Yeah. I'm thinkin' at least four. Maybe six."

"Six?" She laughs. "What'll we do with 'em all?"

"Take care of 'em. Raise 'em. Make 'em better people."

"Better?"

"Better, yeah."

"Is there somethin' wrong with us?"

"Not us. Other people. That's why we need to have kids. To balance things off."

"Oh."

"Sooner the better." He pokes at the Kleenex. "Every time I wear one of these I feel like I'm killin' somethin'."

"Some people never get pregnant."

"That's generally because they've been waitin' for the perfect moment and by the time they figure they're ready, their bodies have forgot how. Or one person has an accident. Or dies. It's too late. That's what I mean. There's no guarantees. If you're gonna do somethin', do it while you can; while you're young, don't sit around thinkin' about it or plannin' for sometime in the future, 'cause there might not be a future."

"Are you sayin' this 'cause of what happened to your brother?"

"I don't wanna talk about my brother. He's got nothin' to do with this."

"It was an accident."

"Sure, it was. Did I say it wasn't?"

"No. I just wanna be clear there's nothin' ..."

"It was an accident. OK? I mean, I wish it hadn't happened, but it did. It was years ago. I still remember it, I can't forget it, it still hurts sometimes, but I've learned to deal with it. At least, I hope I have. Is that clear enough?"

Jenny nods.

"Fine. Let's drop it and move on, OK?"

"OK. So long as you're sure."

"I'm sure. OK?" He kisses her on the forehead.

"And you're happy? With me?"

"Totally. Couldn't be happier."

"OK."

"OK. Hey!" He jumps out of bed. "I've got somethin' for you." He crosses the room, opens a drawer in the dresser. "You know the thing they say about weddings: somethin' old, somethin' new, somethin' borrowed, somethin' blue?"

"Yeah, sort of."

"Whattaya got so far?"

"So far? I don't know. I never thought about it."

"Well, you should. I mean it, it's important. Rituals and such."

"Isn't it just, like, superstition?"

"Maybe. But why take chances? Doesn't cost anythin' and, who knows? Maybe it makes a difference."

"Maybe."

"So, you've got an old dress, yeah? You got it from a used clothing place in town. Somethin' new is the ring. Somethin' borrowed is my boss's car to drive from the wedding to the honeymoon suite at the Radisson in Regina. We're three quarters there. All we need is somethin' blue

..." He withdraws something from the drawer, hides his hands behind his back, slides over the floor to the bed and dangles two blue ribbons in front of her face. "Ta-da!"

"What are those?"

"Somethin' blue. You can use them to tie your hair up."

"You know I don't like to tie my hair up. It makes me feel ... claustrophobic."

"It's only for a few hours. And it's important. For the ritual. You don't want the wedding to be cursed, do you?"

She stares at the ribbons; pokes at them with her fingers. "Can't I wrap them around my wrists instead?"

"No. I want you to wear them in your hair. Doesn't have to be tight. It would please me. The blue snakin' through the blonde. Beautiful, yeah?"

"Snaking? Nice word. Poetic."

"Umm. Besides, just think how sexy it'll be when we get to the hotel and I untie the ribbons and your hair falls over your bare shoulders."

He drags the ribbons slowly up and down her head and across her neck. He pulls the sheet from her chest and tickles her nipples. She lies back and moans softly. He slips the sheet further down to reveal her belly and pubic area. He kisses her breasts and teases the ribbons between her thighs.

"I can use them later to tie your wrists and ankles to the bed."

"You're bad," she says, moaning.

"I am bad. Very bad."

"OK," she whispers. "OK."

She can feel his growing erection against her thigh.

"I love you," she says.

"Love you too, baby."

She grabs his ass and digs in her nails.

～

The house is a small, detached wood and yellow vinyl siding bungalow loomed over by two, two and a half storey semi-detached brick units. There's just enough room on either side to push a medium sized wheelbarrow, maybe. Postage stamp-sized front lawn. A paving stone path, three concrete steps and a small wood landing lead to the door.

"Looks tiny," she says.

"It's what the agent calls a starter upper. We live here a few years, get established, build up some equity, buy somethin' bigger, y'know? Besides, it's got everythin' we need: two bedrooms, cozy living room, combination kitchen/dining room, bathroom with one of those stacked washer/dryer units, half-finished basement, back yard with a bit of lawn and a shed. Updated plumbing and electric. New roof. Easy to care for. I can walk to work so don't need a car. Grocery store within spittin' distance. It's got character, yeah?" Warren waits for an answer that doesn't come. "I think it's got character. Anyway, it's all we can afford right now." Still no reply. "You're not mad or anythin' are you?"

"I'm not mad, no. I guess I just wish I had been more a part of ... you know ... findin' a place for us."

"You're the one who said you wanted to spend time with your folks."

"I know."

"We talked about this. I said come with me, remember? You made the decision to stay. I went along with it 'cause I thought it'd make you happy."

"Yes, and it was sweet of you."

"Uh-huh. And shoppin' around for a house ain't exactly my idea of a good time. Or dealin' with asshole bankers who look at me like I've got two heads when I say I want a mortgage. As it is we were lucky to get this, price of real estate and all. The agent said."

"I believe you."

"I did the best I could. I really did. I'm sorry. I thought you'd like it. Shit."

"You know what? It's fine. It really is. You're right. It is all we need right now. It just didn't fit the picture I had in my head, that's all. I simply have to re-adjust. I mean, I didn't have much more back on the farm, did I? And the house does have character. It looks like a small frosted cake sitting there."

"Yeah? You're sure?"

"Sure I'm sure. Let's go in and take a closer look."

"That's my girl." They load up with suitcases and bags. "And remember, we both picked out the furniture from the catalogue, so ..."

"I'm sure it looks great."

"Yeah, it does. I mean, I had to re-jig some stuff 'cause things didn't quite fit the way we thought, a bit tight and so on. The bed, y'know, is kinda crammed in one corner

...￼" His face and hands work to try and show what he means but Jenny just shoots him a confused look. "Anyway, you'll see. And we can always change the colours of the walls and whatnot if you don't like it. Hell, I can get paint at the store at a discount, right? And wallpaper."

"Stop already, I'm sold," Jenny says, laughing. "C'mon. Gimme the tour."

❧

End of September, warm day, clear sky, a man in faded coveralls stands in the yard and tosses a final handful of feed to the chickens. He drops the plastic bucket, walks across the dirt, leans his arms on top of a fence rail. He pulls an apple from a trouser pocket, bounces it in his palm, rolls it in his fingers, makes a clicking sound with his tongue. The horse trots over, takes the apple from the man's hand. He pats the horse's neck and nose. His wife joins him. They stand there quietly as the horse chews and flicks its tail at flies.

"You figure we should keep him or what?"

"Doesn't make a lot of sense, I guess."

"Probably not, what with Jenny having the twins and such. That'll occupy her time, I think, pretty much. Tough for her to get back and visit."

"She's taken on a load, all right."

"Sounds like things are fine, though, otherwise. Between the two of them, I mean. And the babies. Everyone healthy and happy."

"That what she said?"

"Not in so many words. It's what I gathered. You know what it's like over the phone, never enough time."

"Uh-huh. Well, that's good. I'm glad."

The woman sniffs and sighs. "Horse'll just cost us money. And serve as a reminder."

"Yeah, enough of those around already without payin' to feed a horse no one'll ever ride again."

"Should be easy enough to find him a good home. A family with kids."

"No doubt."

"Still a few of those around."

"Yeah." He gives the horse a gentle push. "Go on," he says. "I got nothin' more for ya."

"In the meantime, maybe we could plan to make a trip to Toronto ourselves, yeah? See our grandchildren before they grow. They don't stay babies long. It'd be nice. I'm sure Jenny would love it."

"Yeah, we should do that. Figure out the best time and all."

"Sure. Doesn't need to be right away. Even Jenny said. They're still in the middle of renovations, as well, so space is tight. You know. We'll talk about it."

"Yeah, we will."

"Good."

The woman chews the inside of her lip and wipes a tear from the corner of an eye. The man maybe sees her or doesn't. He breaks from the fence and ambles slowly toward the barn.

Warren winds between furniture and through the general clutter of the living room floor: toys, magazines, dishes, cutlery, plastic food wrappers, grocery store flyers with discount coupons cut out and scattered over sofa cushions and end tables, baby clothing and so on.

"Jenny," he calls. "Jenny?"

The kitchen is a disaster area, comparable to the living room, maybe worse. The sink is full of dirty dishes that stretch over the entire counter. Scraps of toast, crackers and other foodstuffs litter the floor. Empty soup tins, empty jam jars, empty plastic and Styrofoam containers overflow the blue bin. A garbage can is heaped with disposable diapers. There are baby wipes and tissues. Mops, brooms and dust pans lean uselessly against cupboard doors. The floor is stained and covered in dirt, grime and other miscellaneous filth. Jenny hunches over the table gripping a coffee mug in one hand. Her back heaves sporadically.

"What's up, babe? Everythin' OK?"

Jenny slowly raises her head and tilts her face toward him. Her eyes are red, her cheeks stained with tears, her nose chafed and runny, her breathing short, choppy and interrupted by gasps, hiccups and the need to swallow.

"I'm sorry, Warren," she says. "I'm sorry. I can't do this. I'm not good at it. I'm no good as a mother. I don't know how."

"Don't be silly. You're doin' fine. You're doin' as well as anyone. Remember what the doctor said: babies don't come with an instruction manual, you have to work through it on your own. Trial by fire."

"I'm not workin' through it, Warren. If anythin', I'm gettin' worse. Look around. The place is a total mess. I can't keep up. I'm a lousy housekeeper. I'm a bad wife. I can't stop cryin'. Everytime I think I'm goin' to get somethin' done, one of the twins howls, then the other. They don't stop. I play with them. I rock them. I walk them. I feed them. I change them. Then it starts up again. Nothin' else gets done. Time just disappears."

"You're takin' care of the babies, that's the main thing. The most important. The rest of it doesn't matter. Place is a mess, so what? That's the way it is when you have kids. They take priority. I'd say you're doin' a terrific job."

"You sure?"

"Sure I'm sure."

"The mess doesn't bother you?"

"No! Why should it? It's temporary, yeah? Anyway, what's the big deal? Like I say, the main thing is the babies. They're the ones that need you most right now."

"You're sweet to say that." She sniffs and wipes her nose with the back of a hand.

"I'm not just sayin' it. It's true." He leans in, kisses her on the forehead, stands back and regards her closely. "You get your hair cut?"

Jenny squints, as if thinking; as if trying to remember. She lifts one hand and pats at her head. Her hair is coarse and uneven, like it's been chopped with garden shears.

"Oh yeah. It was getting' in the way. I couldn't stand it, so ..." She forms her hand into a pair of scissors and makes cutting motions with her fingers.

"Uh-huh. Makes sense. Could use a little, you know, here and there." He uses his hands as scissors. "Maybe a comb. Otherwise ..."

"I was sorta desperate. Didn't use a mirror, just chop, chop, chop."

"No, you did fine. It's just hair, right? Grows back. So, we're good here? You feel better?"

"Yeah. Better. Oh ... I saw a mouse today. Here, in the kitchen. I think it was a mouse. There. In front of the fridge. Then it ducked under."

"What—one mouse? That's it? OK, look, I got a couple days off comin' up, we'll set aside a few hours, clean the place up. How's that sound?"

"Might need more than a few hours. Plus a backhoe." She grins and hiccups.

"Then we'll get a backhoe." He grins back at her. "Meantime, I brought home dinner. Chinese." He holds up a plastic bag. "Hungry?"

"No. Tired. I'm tired. The babies are finally asleep. Who knows for how long? I think I need to crash awhile. If I can get a few hours sleep, y'know?"

"Sure. Do that. You can eat later. No problem. I'll just hang here. Maybe go downstairs and work on my little project for a while. You haven't gone down there, have you? And looked?"

"No, of course not. You asked me not to. Though, I am curious."

"Good. Make sure you don't. I want it to be a surprise."

"I know. You're sweet. Thank you, Warren. Really. I love you. You know that. I do."

"I know that. And I love you too. Go to bed. You'll feel better."

Jenny pushes up from the table and drags herself out of the kitchen. Warren follows her with his eyes and waits to hear her climb the stairs. He steps to the fridge, swings the door, grabs a beer and twists off the cap. He carefully sets the cap between his thumb and pointing finger, aims and flicks the cap across the room. It spins and bounces off a far wall. He smiles and gives a nod of approval. He tips the beer to his lips and drinks. He sits at the table, tears into the knotted plastic bag, crushes it, peels the lid from a container of chicken Chow Mein, uses his teeth to tear open a pouch of Soy sauce, squeezes the brown liquid onto the food, rips the paper wrapper from a pair of bamboo chopsticks.

He piles the waste neatly beside him: wadded plastic bag, plastic lid, plastic pouch, paper wrapper, gives it a hard look and very purposefully, very deliberately, uses his forearm to calmly sweep the mess off the table onto the floor.

He laughs to himself, takes another swig of beer and digs into dinner.

～

Late morning. The two of them sit at the kitchen table drinking coffee. The aluminum pot stands between them and they take turns topping up their mugs. The golden lab sniffs and snorts at their feet. The couple discuss the usual things: weather, finances, various shopping lists for when they go into town. They add cream and sugar to their mugs.

"You were restless again last night."

"Yeah."

"You got up. You were awhile. Where'd you go?"

"For a walk. Outside."

"Pretty cold for that. And dark."

"Not so bad. Full moon."

"Every year around this time. Same thing."

"I know."

"It wasn't your fault. It was an accident."

"I know. Doesn't mean I can forget. Or wish it never happened. Or wish I could change it."

"It was a long time ago. You can't go back."

"I know that too. Still, I keep going over the details. In my mind. I keep thinking if a single thing had been different, either happened or didn't, a few minutes or even a few seconds either way."

"You're going to drive yourself crazy."

"Was a night like tonight. We heard a noise from outside. I grabbed my rifle."

"We thought it was a fox after the chickens."

"I went outside to look around. There was nothing. Chickens settled down. I waited. I came back in. Next morning I noticed the lid closed on that busted ice box. I pried it open, and inside ..."

"You couldn't have known."

"Warren's brother, Nathan. Dead. Suffocated. What the hell happened?"

"You know what happened."

"Yeah. They heard the door, they saw the porch light go on. Nathan twisted the chicken's neck, sent Warren home with it while he hid so he could steal another hen when I was gone. He got himself locked inside the ice box all night and that was that."

"That was that. What could you do? What could anyone do?"

"That's where I'm stuck. That's when I think, a few seconds either way, they've got two hens and they're gone. Or no hens and they're gone. Or I catch them, give them a piece of my mind, warn 'em next time I'll call the police. Or I hear the slam of the ice box lid. Or I notice it's shut while I'm there looking around and I find him. Or maybe we got a dog like Boone here at the time and he sniffs 'em out."

"You're going to drive yourself crazy."

"All because they're hungry. Why didn't they just ask? We'd've fed 'em, fer chrissakes. Didn't they know that? Why didn't they know that?"

"There was more going on, don't forget."

"Yeah."

"Police went to the house. Their dad, dead, what? Several weeks they figured? Place a mess. Filthy. Bugs everywhere. Rats. Imagine them living like that. In fear. How were you going to fix all that?"

"Doesn't make it any easier." He takes a sip from his mug and makes a face. "Coffee's cold."

His wife grabs the pot then stops herself. She hangs there until she has her husband's attention.

"What?"

"I spoke with Jenny this morning."

"Yeah? And?"

"She's pregnant."

"Already?"

"Yeah. Doctor said it was unusual so soon, though not unheard of. Jenny joked. Said maybe she was one of those women, y'know? Gets pregnant if a man even looks at her crooked." She smiles and lowers her eyes.

"Otherwise?"

"Not sure. We still haven't visited. I think, maybe ..."

The man stares down at the floor. A shudder ripples his body.

"You cold?"

"No." He sighs. "Not cold. It's something else. Didn't want to tell you. That boy. That boy. I can't help it. He scares me. He scares the living Jesus out of me. I'm sorry, but it's true. Since the time he gave me that look all those years ago, I've been scared of him. Not of anything he did. What he might do. What he's capable of doing."

"Like what? What are you afraid he'll do?"

"I don't know."

The woman places a hand on his and gently squeezes.

"There, there," she says. "There, there."

⁓

Jenny's in the middle of the small bedroom. There's hardly space to move, enclosed as she is by two cribs, a playpen, a small bed where she often lies down to breast feed the twins, a change table littered with new and used diapers, new and used baby wipes, various creams, ointments and powders, a tipped trash can, a second upright trash can and a laundry basket both filled to bursting. Another table displays several miniature photographs of Jenny and the girls, taken by Warren and mounted in ornate frames. A shelving unit is stuffed with odds and ends. The floor is covered with toys, children's books, pieces of clothing, sheets and blankets, tins and bottles, either full, partially full or empty. She stares vacantly at the one wall that contains a single square window. A slatted blind is pulled closed. It doesn't matter. She knows there's nothing to see except darkness anyway as the sunlight is effectively blocked by the neighbouring brick wall.

Maybe she's been standing this way for five minutes, maybe five hours, there's no way to tell for sure.

She wears a man's checked shirt. It's food-stained, loose, rolled at the sleeves, untucked with the bottom few buttons undone. Her jeans are baggy with the legs rolled to her ankles. She's barefoot. Her hair is matted, her eyes are red and teary, her cheeks are flushed, her nose is raw from blowing. Her round bare belly hangs out from the shirt and spills over her belt. She breathes in short jerky gasps. A damp Kleenex twists and shreds between the fingers of one agitated hand.

One of the twins cries from her crib and Jenny's head snaps alert. A small sound of surprise emits from her throat and the Kleenex drops to the floor. She bends to one side and lifts the baby into the air. The baby stretches her mouth open, squints her eyes and howls.

"It's OK, baby, I'm here. Mommy's here. It's OK.

Don't cry." She bounces the child gently in her arms. "You'll wake your sister." Rather than soothe, the remark seems to incite the child. She takes a deep breath and releases a piercing scream that not only sends a shudder through Jenny's body, it rouses the sister who thrashes about in her crib and screams to high heaven.

Jenny transfers the first child to one shoulder and uses a practiced move to scoop the second child and support her against the other shoulder. The girls kick and squirm. They howl in unison, one in each of Jenny's ears.

"There, there," she says. "Are you hungry? Huh? Is that it? Shall I feed you? You wanna be fed, is that it? OK. OK. Just stop screaming, please. Please, stop screaming. I can't think when you both scream like that." She bounces them. They clench their tiny hands. They slap and beat at her chest, neck and face; pull at her hair and ears. They refuse to stop or even slow down. "Do you want the light out, huh? Is it too bright in here? Is that it? You want mommy to turn out the lights?"

Jenny pushes past the furniture, stumbles through debris, inches her way to the door and flips the light switch. The room goes to semi-darkness. The babies don't flinch. If anything they get louder, more restless.

"OK. OK. Mommy will feed you. Just, please, please, be quiet." She eases toward the small bed, peels the two off her chest, lays them on the mattress where they continue to flail, kick and howl like a pair of demons.

"Look," she says. "See? Mommy's getting ready to feed you."

Jenny unbuttons her shirt, slips it off and tosses it at

the foot of the bed. She does the same with her bra. She cups her breasts with her hands and jiggles her nipples in the girls' direction.

"Is this what you want, huh?" She looks down at her breasts. "Oh my God." Her voice trembles. "Is this it? Is this what I've become?" She pinches milk from her nipples. "Is this what I am?"

She drops her hands and rubs her belly. She slowly undoes her belt, unzips her jeans, bends at the waist and slides the pants down her thighs. She straightens, lifts one foot then the other and kicks the jeans to one side. She stands naked, as if transfixed. She runs three fingers through her pubic hair, pulls at her labia, parts the lips and feels for her clitoris. She stops, raises her fingers to eye level and rubs the tips together.

Dry, she thinks. *Dry.*

She claps her hands around her ears to try and drown out the noise of the girls. It's no good. She clenches her eyes and screws up her face. She takes a deep breath, opens her mouth and screams right along with them. Her knees give way and she crumples to the floor. She sobs and cries. Her screams choke to muffled moans and whimpers. She crawls backward through the clutter, past the cribs until the soles of her feet bump against the playpen. She twists her body, climbs her hands up two wooden bars, grabs the top rail, tips the playpen and pulls it over top of her. She presses her body into one corner of the cage, snatches the edge of a pink blanket, drags it close and buries her head beneath it. Her eyes squeeze shut as she feels the walls close in around her. She continues to gasp and whimper like a trapped, wounded animal. The babies continue to howl in the background.

～

Warren barely breaks stride as he saunters from the sidewalk onto the paving stones that lead to the front porch. He ascends the three steps, crosses the wooden boards, and enters the house.

"Jenny!" he calls. "Jenny?"

He takes the stairs to the second floor two at a time. When he comes back down, his pace has slowed considerably. He hits each step in turn, flat-footed. There's a slight smile on his face and he whistles an unrecognizable tune under his breath. He winds his way to the kitchen and sits at the table. He holds two blue ribbons in his hands which he ravels and unravels and tugs and stretches between his fingers. They're the same two ribbons Jenny had used to tie her hair for their wedding.

He lays the ribbons on the table alongside a pile of newsprint flyers, a pair of scissors, a roll of tape, and goes to the basement. He returns holding an exact small-scale replica of their house, which he's constructed using cardboard and balsa wood. He drops the model next to the ribbons and searches out a suitable-sized box in the pantry. Finding one, he places it on the table with the rest of the materials. He picks up the model and gazes at it appreciatively. He leans his eye closer to study the second floor master bedroom. In the glass window squares he's pasted a photo of Jenny in her wedding dress, blankly staring out, smiling, her hair tightly tied with blue ribbons.

Warren places the model gently inside the box and uses wadded newsprint as padding to keep it from getting damaged in transit. He closes the box and tapes down the seams. Using a black magic marker from his shirt pocket, he prints a name and address in the centre of the box: that of Jenny's parents in Saskatchewan.

Dear mom and dad ..., he whispers, and chuckles.

He doesn't bother to supply a return address. They'll know who it's from before they even open it, he reckons.

As insurance, he grabs the ends of the tangled blue ribbons and dangles them in the air. He notices some strands of Jenny's hair knotted in places and leaves them, for effect. Otherwise, he does his best to flatten the ribbons by dragging them between the tips of his thumb and index finger. Somewhat satisfied, he winds the ribbons taut around the box. He ties a knot at the top and uses the excess length to fashion a pretty bow by curling the ends with the scissor blade's edge. He lifts the package in front of his face to admire his handiwork.

He checks the time on his cell and figures he can just make it before closing. He hurries outside, heads to the nearest post office, sends the package on its way and returns home. He cracks himself a beer and takes a hard, cold look around.

"What a mess," he says, more or less to himself. "What a pig sty."

He empties his beer over the kitchen table and bounces the bottle across the floor. He turns, and goes to the foot of the stairs.

"Jenny," he calls softly. "Jenny? It's me." There's no response. He taps at the step riser with the toe of his work shoe. "I'm coming up. Jenny? I'm coming up the stairs. Is that OK?"

He grabs the railing and hauls himself upward. Each stair creaks beneath his weight.

⌇

The funeral was a small affair, with a handful of friends and relatives returned to the house for refreshments and conversation. Jenny is in close conversation with her mother. Warren stands nearby, within earshot, drinking a Coke.

"I don't understand, mom. How he could do this. Was anything troubling him? Did you notice anything wrong?"

"Not really, dear. I mean, he'd been quieter recently, more reclusive. If that was even possible. You know your father. He was never much for talking. Or sharing his feelings."

"Had anything happened recently? Anything that might have upset him?"

"No, I don't think so."

"And you found him."

"Yes. His body was hanging from a rope in the barn."

"It must've been horrible for you."

Jenny's mother rocks her head and wipes a tear from her eye with the back of a hand.

"And the police didn't find anything unusual?"

"You mean signs of foul play? No. Though, there was one thing ..." She takes a breath and blows her nose in a Kleenex. "It seems he made a small fire in the barn and burned something. The police don't know what. Apparently he must've taken his time, and was very thorough in making sure that, whatever it was, it was completely reduced to ashes."

"That's odd," Jenny says. "I wonder what it was, and why he would do such a thing?"

"Did he leave a note?" Warren asks, over Jenny's shoulder. "They say suicides often leave a note."

"No. There was nothing like that."

"So, nothing he said, no hint, no explanation whatsoever?"

"I'm afraid not. It's all very mysterious." She looks from Warren to Jenny. "But, again ... your father."

"Uh-huh. Do you think maybe he was depressed about something? He could've been and you wouldn't even know. I didn't know."

"You?"

"Yes. I thought it was because I couldn't handle being a mother. I couldn't do anything. I was a wreck, the house was a wreck. And poor Warren ..." She takes his hand in her hers and draws him closer. "Then, when we got the news about dad, he decided to take matters into his hands. He pretty much dragged me to the doctor kicking and screaming. Turns out I was going through post-partum depression. Who'd've thought?"

"And now?"

"Half the battle is knowing. I'm on medication, and that seems to help. Meanwhile, Warren is my prince. Once we found out, he went through the house like a white tornado. Cleaned and scrubbed every room, top to bottom, so that it's spotless. Now, he's planning to put a bed and bathroom in the basement. You'll be able to come and visit if you want. Or stay, if you like. If you find the farm is too much for you."

"It sounds lovely. I'll think about it. I wouldn't want to impose." She looks at Warren.

"No problem, we'd like that. Of course, we're still in the planning stages. And there'll be the new baby to think about." Warren puts his arm around Jenny's shoulder and gives her a squeeze.

"Yes, that's true. Well, I should see to my other guests. It's so nice you could come, really. And bring the twins. They're adorable." She begins to walk away, and stops. "Oh, I just remembered, there was one other thing that was unusual."

"What was that?" Warren asks.

"He had a scrap of thin blue ribbon wound around one wrist. I'm sure I don't know what that was all about, or where he would've gotten it. He wasn't one for wearing that sort of thing. Adornments. Well ..." She shrugs and smiles. "Look at the pair of you, so in love. It's wonderful."

She leaves to go and mingle with the rest of the group.

Jenny slips her arm around Warren's waist and leans her head on his chest. She places her other hand on her round belly.

"The baby's kicking," she says. "Feel."

The pair gaze into each other's eyes and smile.

THE MISSING PERSON'S TALE

*In which a woman's search for freedom takes
her on a road fraught with danger and unexpected
twists and turns, ending ultimately
with a sort of redemption.*

It's a hot, dry summer day. Reuben manoeuvres the truck slow and easy alongside the highway. Tires churn a lazy dust cloud from the stone and gravel shoulder. No need to rush. He doesn't clock out for another four hours and what he's looking for isn't about to go anywhere. Stay focused, that's the key. First indication is the dark swoop and flap of crows gathered in the distance. A murder of crows, Reuben thinks. What it's called. Perversely poetic, given the circumstances. Like a wake of buzzards or an ostentation of peacocks. A skulk of foxes. A nuisance of cats. Funny. He pulls up beside, applies the brakes, shifts into park, steps out of the cab. The crows fire a sidelong glare then it's back to business: Tear into the bloodied entrails. The prey, a fat raccoon, appears reasonably whole and in still-decent shape, despite the spill of guts. Unusual on the highway. The victims are generally struck during the night then continue to be run over repeatedly by further passing vehicles. By the time Reuben discovers them, they're a tread-worn pulpy mess.

Different story if they bounce off to the shoulder or land in the grass beyond. This guy was close enough to the asphalt's edge that he managed to escape suffering too much damage. Apart from death, of course.

Meanwhile, the crows.

Reuben slips into a pair of work gloves and hauls a wide flat shovel from two hooks screwed to the wood slat side of the truck bed. He approaches the carcass, checks for traffic, bangs the end of the shovel against the asphalt, waves an arm and whistles through his teeth. The crows lift off. Reuben settles a corner of the shovel under one end of the animal and with a practiced hand slides and twists it onto the flat face, into the air and onto the truck in one slick motion. He divides the bed right and left, separates the general splatter from the more intact casualties.

He returns the shovel to its hooks, the gloves to a back pocket, jumps in the truck and grinds onto the highway. A portable CD player sits on the seat beside him. He grooves to Neil Young's *Cinnamon Girl*, rocks his shoulders, beats the steering wheel with his fingers. Doesn't take long before he spots what looks like the body of a deer nestled in the gravel ditch. He noses the truck to a stop, gets out, makes a quick inspection. It's a buck, all right, and judging by its eight-inch antler spread, about eighteen months old. Reuben also estimates it weighs in the neighbourhood of 130-140 pounds. There's no sign of blood anywhere on the hide. Probably hit hard and died of a broken neck. Reuben squats and strokes the animal's rib cage. Beautiful creature, he thinks. A rotten shame. Nothing to be done, though. He grabs two ankles with one hand, two with the other, gives a grunt, pushes up with his legs and swings the deer around his neck. He stands there and takes a breath in through the nose and out through the mouth.

Reuben strikes an impressive sight posed there, the buck folded around his neck. He's in his early thirties, about six feet tall, muscular with strong arms and hands. He sports a close-cropped beard, has brown skin, hazel eyes, roman nose and lanky black hair that falls from under his ball cap down to his collar.

He walks to the rear of the truck, spins and allows the buck to slide onto the bed. He reaches in, tucks his hands under the animal's ribs and rolls it further to the front to make room. There were bound to be other unfortunates before his shift ended.

He wipes the dust from his hands onto his jeans and withdraws a cigarette pack from a shirt pocket. He taps a roll-your-own from the box, lights up with a silver Zippo, sucks short puffs and inhales deeply, allowing the smoke to settle in his lungs. He blows out through pursed lips and repeats the process. Done with the joint, he flicks the roach, pulls a thermos from a lunch box and pours himself a coffee. He leans his body on the driver's door, one knee bent, the foot lifted off the ground, the boot heel grinding the paint. Through the open window, he listens to Neil wail: "Everybody knows this is nowhere." He drinks his coffee.

A clash of bucks, he thinks.

A fesnyng of ferrets.

It has to end. What has to end? She isn't sure, so, everything, obviously. What other choice is there, one thing part and parcel with the rest? How has she allowed it to go on this long? That's the bigger million dollar question she asks herself over and over, though in her heart-of-hearts she knows the answer. She's weak. She's a coward. She's a loser. She's what her mother always says: lack of character; lack of backbone; lack of self-confidence/self-respect; lack of moral fibre; lack of inner resources. That and the medications, of course. Meant to keep her mentally and emotionally balanced. *Un*-disturbed. Help her avoid a nervous breakdown in a public space; avoid causing embarrassment to herself and others; avoid drinking herself half to death: *One hour at a time, one day at a time, one step at a time.* Instead, exist as a sleep walker, a pushover for the first kind word, the first available offer. Not to mention a pricey weekly shrink who quizzes her on where she buys her shoes, who does her hair, what particular shade of red is her lipstick. And like a fool she answers. A sucker born every minute. Not to mention regular AA meetings that make her want to puke. *Don't quit five minutes before the miracle happens.* Fuck you, she replies. Fuck you and the horse you rode in on. In her head she says this; what she thinks; what she believes, yet, keeps her mouth shut, continues to attend religiously, nods her head obediently: yes, master; yes, master. *We are only as sick as our secrets.* And she admits she is a seriously sick puppy. Yes, all of this and more. Though most especially a coward, as ... what will she do? Where shall she go? How will she end it?

The answer to the first question is simple—who gives a rat's ass? Whether type memos or wash dishes it all adds up to the same dull monotony in the final analysis: work to live or live to work makes no difference. Eat, shit, sleep, maybe go bowling once a week. First honey, then the knife. *C'est fini!* The answer to question number two? North! Isn't that where everyone goes when they want to get lost? Not south where it's nice and warm and sunny and anyone and their mother is happy to follow you just because. No, north, where there's always a fair chance you'll freeze your tits off or be eaten by ravenous beasts, so, goodbye Charlie! Answer to the third question? Being a coward, end it in a cowardly fashion, meaning ... not with a bang but a whimper. No ending, no closure, no nothing. Not a note, not an email, not a text, no attempt at an explanation of any sort, because what explanation is there beyond the fact she is a royal pain in the butt to everyone around her and a complete and total screw up?

How else explain living with a man she doesn't love, never loved, never will love and remains with because he happened to take an interest in her several years prior and said those magic words: "Will you marry me?" And promised *you* alone, forsaking all others for eternity? Or having an affair with a married man she doesn't find particularly attractive either mentally, physically or personality-wise, does not find sexy in any way whatsoever and must (even) stifle her laughter when he undresses

—something to do with the shape and/or colour of his penis—is years too old for her, yet agreed simply because he said he desired her? He "desired" her. Never mind the man is her boss, fer chrissakes. Or that to get her shrink back on track she devises mock confessions where she says she enjoys finger painting with her feces or has fantasies about sucking the cocks of young black choirboys or being finger-fucked on the sacred altar steps by an arthritic priest or has dreams of nailing her mother's forehead to the ornamental teak dining room table. Interesting, the shrink goes, tapping her bottom lip with the eraser end of a pencil. Tell me more. Yeah, the more outlandish and horrific, the better. Meanwhile, omit items such as self-loathing, fear of intimacy and dissatisfaction with body image—breasts too small, ass too big or vice versa—issues which have become commonplace, almost normal, in our freak-obsessed society, talked to death by Oprah and others of her ilk, plus experts in psychobabble: Dr. Phil, Dr. Gupta, Dr. Ruth, Dr. Oz, and so, a colossal bore. Omit, as well, the items where she induces vomiting and cuts herself with a steak knife on her thighs and belly. Little more than a weak cry for help, yes, and, not so bad, she guesses, really, in the grand scheme of things, if it weren't all so pathetic, lame and ultimately stereotypical. *We are only as sick as our secrets.* This being merely the tip of the cracked iceberg, just throw together a suitcase, a backpack and get the hell out of Dodge, pronto! Who'd miss her, anyway?

"Desired." That one word, she knows. If she could only desire something or someone. Instead ...

The truck bed drags beneath the weight of road kill. Reuben cruises, his foot heavier on the gas with the knowledge of another day's work almost complete. By habit he continues to scan the surrounding area, highway ahead, lake to the left, to the right a blur of black spruce and alder. Beyond this, swamp. Higher up, white pine and trembling aspen. A few more kilometres and ... what was that? He catches something out the corner of his eye, off the shoulder, part way into the trees. He cranks the wheel, hits the brakes, shifts into reverse. He cuts the engine, hops out and scouts the area. Maybe something, maybe nothing. Then, there it is. Body of a woman lying face up on the ground. She wears a man's baseball cap with a Blue Jays logo on it, a blue denim blouse, dark blue cotton hiking shorts, one foot has a brown sandal on it, the other foot is bare. An oval patch of blood stains the right side of her blouse. Most likely hit by the headlight of a passing car, Reuben figures. Tore into her. She flew a distance, bounced, crawled; eventually gave in to the pain, the exhaustion, and rolled over. That, or she was hit, knocked a mile, landed on a sharp branch or rock, bounced, crawled, rolled over. Definitely crawled as there are drag marks in the dirt and grass. The missing sandal landed or twisted free several yards behind her. Also a backpack situated in close proximity.

Reuben regards her, like: This is not your regular sack of potatoes. As he considers possibilities, a snake appears, slithers over the woman's arm and coils itself in the middle of her chest. The snake is grey with a row of large rounded black blotches down the centre of the back, three smaller rows of alternating spots down each side and the immediately recognizable vertical pupils. A massasauga rattler. Poisonous and seeming pretty cocky for a creature on the threatened species list. Reuben crouches, gives the snake a gentle nudge with the back of his hand to move it along, lifts the woman under her knees and neck and straightens. Light as a feather, he thinks. He carries her to the truck, instinctively goes to the tailgate, stops, regards the woman, regards the steam of carcasses, turns, sidles to the passenger side, opens the door, slumps her into the seat, carefully shuts her in. He retrieves the backpack, jumps into the driver's seat, drops the pack at the woman's feet. He uses two fingers to remove a CD from the player and snap it back into its jewel case. He drums the CD holder, puts his hand on one plastic case then another. He makes a soft sound in his chest, chooses a new disc and sets it playing. It's Lucinda Williams: *Car Wheels On a Gravel Road.*

He lifts the gearshift toward him, drags it into drive and hits the gas.

~

When it comes down to the nitty-gritty, backed into a corner, balls to the wall, strange how few things one really needs to pack up and go. She climbs into her beater Ford Escort hatchback, winds her way through mid-morning traffic to the 400 north and doesn't pull off the highway until she hits Barrie. She gasses up, checks the oil and wiper fluid, cleans the windows and empties the floor of city detritus: used parking vouchers, empty plastic water bottles, paper coffee cups, fast-food wrappers, bags and so on. Having seen too many cop shows where the person of interest is tracked through use of a debit or credit card, she pays the station attendant cash. Of course, these same shows tell us that a person can't be reported missing to police until 24 hours have passed. Turns out this is bogus. Especially if the missing person is mentally unstable and/or there's fear of self-harm. She certainly qualifies on both these scores.

She bounces into a TraveLodge, arms herself with a basic provincial highway map plus a handful of tourist information brochures, finds a local Tim Hortons, orders a coffee and toasted cinnamon raisin bagel and sits and peruses the material. Sault Ste. Marie, she nods. Why not? She knows nothing about the place aside from the fact it has a romantic ring to it—the Soo. The Soo. She repeats the word aloud several times, mantra-like, intending to imbue it with a sort of mythic quality. The Soo. Besides, if it doesn't work out—the Soo—there are plenty more places further north: Thunder Bay, Rainy River, Kenora, Weagamow Lake, Sachigon Lake ...

Plenty of wide open space in which to disappear and start over again. *Tabula Rasa*. A clean slate. Just drive, he said. Who said? Steve Taylor. Jack Nicholson. Robert Creeley. Something about darkness surrounding us and what can we do against it. Something about buying a car. A goddamn big car. "drive, he sd, for christ's sake, look out where yr going." Or not.

From what dark swirl has she dragged these fragments of ephemera? She shakes her head, reads her brochures and chews on a bite of bagel.

～

Reuben heats water in a large metal pot on the stove. As the water nears the boiling point he squirts in a shot of green dishwashing liquid, removes the pot from the element, tests the temperature with a dipped finger, drops in a clean washcloth and sponge, carries the pot a few feet and sets it on a metal stool seat. He unbuttons his cuffs and rolls his sleeves. The woman is laid out on the kitchen table. A blue rubber mat cushions her body against the wood tabletop. Her head rests on a small blue pillow. She is perfectly still. The ball cap is gone as is the sandal, already discarded into a heavy-duty, black plastic bag along with the other sandal and the backpack. Reuben sets to work. He releases the woman's belt buckle, unsnaps and unzips her shorts, slides the shorts and panties as a single unit down her legs, tosses them into the plastic bag. He unsnaps her denim blouse, notices it sticks to her skin where the blood has dried. He soaks the area with the hot, soapy water, allows it to sit a minute, carefully peels the material away. The bra snap is in front, making it a simple job to undo, remove one arm then the other from both garments simultaneously, give her upper torso a slight lift, subtract the bra and blouse, crush them into a ball and deposit them in the bag along with the rest.

A cursory glance reveals the woman's otherwise pallid skin randomly stained by pinkish-red bruises tinged with purple. Reuben pokes at one or two almost absent-mindedly. He bends at the waist, lays an elbow on the table and studies the gash in the woman's side. He traces the outline with his fingertips. A clean cut, he thinks. Not wide, but deep. He sponges the entire area, squeezes water from the sponge into the pot, repeats the process until he's satisfied the dried blood is removed. He goes on to wash the rest of the woman's body, sponging her ribs, chest, breasts, under her armpits, over her shoulders, down her arms. He uses the washcloth to scrub her hands and fingers; her neck, face and ears. He erases any trace of make-up, which is minimal, anyway. There's no polish on her nails, either fingers or toes.

He dumps the dirty water down the sink, rinses the sponge and washcloth, refills the pot straight from the hot water tap this time and returns to the woman. She fits perfectly comfortable on the table, with a few inches to spare on either end and at the sides. This is a good thing, thinks Reuben, to be comfortable. He guesses she's five-three or five-four. Narrow build, perhaps too much so, with bony hips that look sharp enough to cut a man in the throes, do real damage, if he wasn't careful. Reuben holds the sponge above the woman's belly and allows it to hover there. Something has caught his attention. There are pale thin scars located on her flesh below the navel and across her abdomen, which continue in almost ladder-like patterns, rung by rung, to halfway down her thighs. The scars are healed, so obviously not due to the recent accident. Reuben presses a tip of the sponge against one scar and rubs, as if to wash it away. It doesn't. He takes a deep breath and releases it slowly. He dips the sponge, squeezes it, knocks off the excess moisture and returns to the task at hand.

He sponges her belly, hips, thighs, the pubic mound. He notes the hair is light brown here while on her head the hair is a richer, darker brown with traces of red, suggestive of a visit or visits to a salon. He gently parts her thighs and wipes the labial lips: *minora* and *majora*. He sponges her legs, which are slim, firm and slightly bowed. He pays particular attention to her knees as there are small scrapes from crawling along the ground. He clears away traces of dirt, grime, blood, grass stains and other foreign matter. He switches to the washcloth for her feet, takes his time, being sure to get between and clean each toe individually. He uses his thumbs through the wet cloth to massage the balls of her feet, the soles and heels. He rinses the cloth several times.

He turns the woman over to reveal more bruising. He sponges her up and down: calves, backs of thighs, buttocks, lower back, upper back, shoulders, until her skin gleams. Once complete, he flips her again and covers her with a plain white sheet. He refreshes the water a final time in order to wash her hair. He pours shampoo into his hands, massages it into her scalp, builds up a lather and rinses her hair clean. He rubs it dry with a terrycloth bath towel and combs it out across the blue pillow.

He slips the comb into his pants pocket, carries the pot to the sink, empties the water, rinses the sponge, the washcloth, the pot, places it all in the dish rack, rolls down his sleeves, buttons the cuffs, goes to the fridge, grabs a bottle of beer, twists the cap, spins the cap onto the sink, takes a healthy swig, wanders past the woman into the living room and stretches out on the couch. He picks up the TV remote and hits the power button. The weather station comes on. No change for tomorrow. Hot and dry through the weekend. Zero percent chance of precipitation. Sweet.

Espanola, the woman reads. Population 6,000. Notable facts? In 2001 the town set a record for the longest continuous ice hockey game: three days. This record later broken and broken again, as all records are meant to be broken in time. Was home to the TV series *Adventures in Rainbow County* featuring Lois Maxwell, who later became Miss Moneypenny in the James Bond films. Also home to Domtar Pulp and Paper Mill, one of the most stringent zero-emissions pulp bleaching processes in the world. This, after a toxic spill in the early 1980s killed fish by the thousands in the Spanish River. Impressive, thinks the woman, though it can't erase the mill's stench which continues to dance through the town and surrounding area depending upon which way the wind blows. Also used as a German prisoner of war camp during WWII. Huh, who'd've guessed, way up here?

It's late afternoon and the woman decides to celebrate her impending freedom by having a small drink at the local. She's on meds, but it's a low dose and how much can it hurt? There'll be AA in the Soo—there's AA every-where: *Be part of the solution, not the problem*—and she can get back to her routine. She sits at the bar and orders a dry martini with olives. The bartender tells her it's Happy Hour and for an extra buck, she can make it a double. A double it is, says the woman. To Lois Max-well—shaken not stirred! She finishes the first and or-ders a second.

A guy half in shadow perches on a stool in one cor-ner of the bar. He's in his mid to late forties, heavy-set, bit of a paunch, wears a brown suede sports jacket, bolo tie, white Levis shirt, blue jeans, cowboy boots. He nurs-es a beer and keeps his eye on the woman as she parts her lips and uses her teeth to nibble an olive from the plastic spear. Well, he thinks, why not? Better to be shot as a wolf than live as a sheep. He picks up the remains of his beer and walks over. Hi, he says, grinning. Inter-ested in some company? And if I said no? I'd be dis-appointed. Ah, that's so sad. Why, because you'd miss the pleasure of my sharp wit and sparkling personality? She recognizes the effusive effect the booze has on her and she enjoys it. A sort of Blanche DuBois feeling: I've always depended upon the kindness of strangers, and so on. Half in the bucket; warm and silky. Something like that, he says. The woman pulls a face. Well, we can't have that now, can we? Please, be seated. Though I must warn you that I'm leaving soon. Uh-huh? Me too. Where you headed? The Soooooo. She drags the word out for the sound. Any particular reason? Do I need one? I guess not. She takes his left hand and examines it. Wedding ring? Yep. Kids? Three. Wanna see pictures? He reaches for his wallet and she stops him. S'OK. A no bullshit kind of guy, is that it? Oh, plenty of bullshit, just not about that. You're funny. She spears the final olive into her mouth. I was thinking about ordering up some wings or something. You wanna join me? Big spender. That was a *fer instance*. Order what you want. Steak, seafood, vegetarian ...? No, wings are good. I like wings. I like 'em spicy hot. Good. Me too. Really hot. Fantastic. Suicide it is. Meantime, you need a top up? He indicates her empty glass. Yeah, though I better switch to white wine. Why? You look terrific in a martini. Haha, thass hilarious. Good one. You mean, like, drowning not waving, huh? She takes a deep breath, plugs her nose with a hand, bulges her eyes and cheeks, gives a weak wave with the other hand, sinks her head and shoulders.

The man isn't sure how to respond. He looks at her curiously. No, I mean, like it suits you. Or you suit it. The way you toy with the olives before you eat them. Sexy, slightly dangerous. Oh, I see. Smooth, she says. Very smooth. OK, one more martini, plus wings, then it's *toodle-oo*, off to the Soooooo S'aright? No pressure, no strings, no hanky-panky. The man throws his hands in the air and crosses his heart with a thumb, like: Wouldn't dream of it! *And* ... I pay my own way. No need, he says. I have a company expense account. She taps a finger on the bar. I-pay-my-own-way. S'aright?

The man smiles and shrugs. S'aright. He twirls a finger and the bartender drops two fresh drinks. Easy as that.

⌁

She manages to open her eyes a crack and attempts to make sense of her surroundings. Her eyelids blink heavily, like malfunctioning venetian blinds. Her head is foggy and her vision is blurred. She knows she's lying on her back. She knows this. She knows that directly above her the plastic blades of a ceiling fan spin in a creepishly retarded fashion. She doesn't feel the slightest movement of air and wonders what's the point? On the other hand, she doesn't feel much of anything, neither too hot nor too cold nor too hard nor too soft. The single term that sticks is: comfortable. She feels comfortable. Though she's uncertain as to what this means. She just is.

She's somewhat aware of music playing faintly in the background. Voice of someone singing. Willie Nelson, maybe. The lyrics are difficult to make out and the title of the tune eludes her.

There seems to be something happening in the region of her upper left arm, a pressure. She drops her chin and tries to focus her vision in that direction. The figure of a snake wrapped around her bicep captures her attention and she wonders if it isn't a piece of jewellery or a decoration of some sort and, if so, how did it get there? She wonders if maybe she isn't reliving a past life experience where she was Queen Cleopatra or the goddess Isis? Though, in this case, the snake isn't gold; it's grey and stares intently at her through vertical pupils while a slender forked tongue darts in and out of its fanged mouth.

Apparently, we're not in Kansas anymore, Toto.

She allows her head to roll further right. Her eyes are met with a low rise of white breasts peaked by two brown nipples. Beyond this, a glimpse of knobby knees and bare toes, at the end of which she spots a big black crow patrolling her feet, its wings alternately spreading and folding, its black head bobbing behind an animated black beak. Further right, higher up, a man looms over her. He wears an Indian war bonnet. His face is striped with paint. A necklace comprised of beads, bones and feathers hangs from his neck. He holds one arm in the air and shakes an egg-shaped rattle in his fist. His chest is bare except for more painted stripes. The man chants something in a language she can't understand. She follows the line of his breastbone downward and discovers he's naked below the waist as well as above. He holds his erection with one hand and guides it slowly, gently inside her open wound. She wants to raise her own hand to say no; stop, but she's unable to make a move; unable to say a word or make a sound. The man thrusts his pelvis rhythmically against her hip, slides his cock in and out; harder, faster. His chants turn to moans. She doesn't feel him come inside her; doesn't feel his cock withdraw, though she assumes as much, given his spent expression. He squeezes out a further thick spray of semen and rubs it into her thighs, stomach and breasts.

Is she dreaming, she wonders? Is she dead? Is she

dreaming she's dead? How does that ancient Japanese story go? A man dreams he's a butterfly dreaming he's a man? The old chicken or egg dilemma, as: What came first? Or a stone so heavy even God can't lift.

One hour at a time, one day at a time, one step at a time.

Bit late for that now, she thinks, and, is it humanly possible to cram another archetypal image into this one fucking scene?

It is Willie Nelson. He croons from somewhere in the foggy background: la-la, something, something … "redemption and leaving things behind" … something … "Mendocino County line …" something, something, la-la … whatever …

It's all too much. Her head hurts. She drops off.

⌒

She knows she's had too much to drink and shouldn't be driving. You're in no shape, the man told her. Besides, what's your hurry, we just met? Have another drink. We'll get a room and crash for the night. Separate beds.

Right. Been there, done that, bought the T-shirt. Wasn't it Dorothy Parker who said, three drinks I'm under the table, four I'm under the host? No, better (safer) to hit the road. There was still some light and it was only about two hours and change to Sault Ste. Marie where she could check into a cozy motel room with a cozy bed and a cozy hot shower all to herself. The main thing? Stay alert: hands on the wheel, eyes on the road, keep to the speed limit. Not much chance of a road block, though she doesn't want to give a passing cop any reason to pull her over. She lowers the window, sucks in the evening air and gives her head a shake.

She turns on the headlights as she nears the outskirts of Massey. About midpoint to Blind River, she feels the front passenger side tire blow. The car veers to the right, careens off the asphalt, across the gravel shoulder and bounces toward the trees. The woman manages to guide the car into what might be a motorbike or ATV dirt trail and pumps the brakes to a slow halt.

Fuck, she says. Fucking hell! Why does this have to happen to me? Why now? She reaches for her backpack, unzips a compartment, fishes for a plastic medicine container. Her hands shake as she pops an Ativan. One per night and otherwise as needed. This is definitely a time of need, she thinks, and pops another. She feels her heart race. She considers her options and realizes none of them are good. She unzips another compartment, takes out a Blue Jays' baseball cap and pulls it on her head. Of all things, why had she packed this, her husband's cap? Meanwhile, she'd stashed her cell phone turned off in the top drawer of her bedside table, scotch taped to her wedding ring, likely to remain there undiscovered for days, if not months. Stupid!

She hauls the backpack out of the car, slips her arms through the straps, treks to the highway, stands there and considers: walk or hitch? If she walks, she estimates she can make it to Blind River in two hours or less. That is, if she's not eaten by bears or abducted, raped and murdered by a psychopathic serial killer. The possibility of attack by a serial killer only more inviting if she sticks out her thumb. After all, the highways are alive with the sound of bloodshed, right? THE EYEBALL KILLER. THE SHOE FETISH SLAYER. THE VAMPIRE OF SACRAMENTO. THE MIDNIGHT MARAUDER. THE WEEPY-VOICED KILLER. THE GREEN RIVER KILLER. THE BOSTON STRANGLER.

At least, that's what the television shows would have us believe. Two or three serial killers brought to justice each night of the week whereas evidence shows there are only about 30-50 active types in the entire country at any given time. Never mind that, while violent crime has increased by over 600 per cent in the past ten years on TV, it has decreased by about thirty per cent in real life. Facts that should set the woman's mind more or less at ease, though they don't. And how do these monsters rate such romantic nicknames? Do the killers themselves create them? No, they are conveniently provided by members of the media. Or the law enforcement agencies. THE BUTTERMILK BLUEBEARD. THE LIPSTICK MURDERER. POGO THE CLOWN. JACK THE FUCKING RIPPER.

She pictures her mother reading about her in a missing person's blurb on the back of a cereal box. Or on a flashing screen in the subway. She thinks about being the unlucky one out of one hundred, wrong place, wrong time, picked up, violated, her severed parts bagged in plastic, wrapped in duct tape and scattered along miles of lake shore. What did she read about Blind River in the brochure? The discovery of uranium in 1955, sure. What else? Oh yeah, in 1991 an elderly couple was shot and killed at the local rest stop just off the highway. The case was profiled on NBC TV's *Unsolved Mysteries*: "The killer may still be among us!" Shit! Her hands continue to shake. She feels the terrors entering her body. She reaches behind and pulls out another pill bottle. She gives the label a look: Hey doll, she says. Do your magic. She takes a Haloperidol, swallows, starts walking.

About an hour in, a car pulls over. A man calls through the open window. Hey, what happened? Are you OK? Where's your car? She bends to get a better look. It's the man from the bar. What happened? he repeats. The woman keeps mum. C'mon, get in. He reaches across and opens the door. She swings around, climbs inside, clutches the backpack on her lap. She shuts the door. Again the man asks, what happened? Flat tire, she says. A ways behind. We can go back, he says. Change the tire. I was already riding the spare, she says. Uh-huh. You OK? She nods.

He lifts the lid of the storage container that separates the bucket seats to reveal a small bottle of Jack Daniels. Take a drink, he says. It'll settle you. He hits the gas pedal and the car lurches onto the highway. *Alcoholism is an equal opportunity destroyer*, she mumbles. What? Nothing. A joke. She takes a swig from the bottle, then another. She passes it to the man who does the same. Are you in the habit of picking up strange women on the road? Not so strange. I recognized you. Her back stiffens at this. She slowly unzips a lower compartment of the backpack and slides her hand inside. She grips the wood handle of a steak knife. What do mean, she says, recognized me? You know. Your general shape. Five-three or four, slim. The blue hiking shorts, sandals. Your ankles. My ankles? Yeah, thin, slightly bowed. I could tell it was you. Pretty observant. Part of the job. Sales, y'know? Gotta keep your eyes open. Though the baseball cap threw me. I never would've thought. Have another shot. Do you good.

The bit about the ankles is perhaps slightly more than she can handle. It goes beyond mere casual observation so far as she's concerned; it borders on intimacy. It approaches observation with intent. She accepts the bottle and drinks. Her brain is on fire, yet she can barely stay awake. Her head drops then snaps to attention. Where's the seat belt? she blurts. Why doesn't the alarm sound? The buzz, buzz, buzz. The seat belt issue is suddenly all-important to her. Deadly important. She's unsure why. Meanings within meanings and so on. Accumulation of events. You're sitting on it, he says. I do it up so I can pile shit in the front seat. Product and such. Display folders.

The woman scans the inside of the car. There's nothing. Makes it easier. Yeah, I bet it does, just go down, open his pants and perform the obligatory blow-job. Or else he climbs on top, hikes her skirt, lowers her panties and ... Bob's your uncle. Nothing to interfere. Here, let me release it so you can buckle up. His hand fumbles for the catch and brushes against her hip and ass. She yanks the knife from the bag and lunges at him across the seat. She presses her face to his and holds the knife to his throat. What are you doing? he says. What does it look like? This isn't funny. It's not supposed to be. What's the

matter with you? The matter with me? What's the matter
with you? Not exactly what you were expecting, huh?
What are you, crazy or something? Put that knife away.
I'll put it away all right. I'll shove it through your gullet.

She's close enough he can smell her boozy breath. Get
off me! Get off me, you drunk bitch! I'm tryin' to drive.
He shoves her away and she flies back at him. You wanna
piece of me, she snarls. You wanna fuck me up good and
proper, huh? Is that it? You're crazy, he screams. You're
crazier than a shithouse rat. You better believe it, pal.
Now tell me, what does the name Charles Albright mean
to you, huh? How about David Berkowitz? Or Ricardo
Caputo? What? I don't know what you're talking about.
Sit down, fer chrissakes. Put the knife away. I can't see
the road. She keeps in his face. Ted Bundy? Gary Ridg-
way? Huh? Ring a bell? How about a non-descript, late
model, four-door sedan, blue or green, with out-of-prov-
ince license plates? How about an average-looking travelling salesman with a wife, three kids and a dog living in
the suburbs and a penchant for killing prostitutes? And
I'll give you a hint—it's not a joke. I don't know what
you're talking about. I offered you a ride, that's it. He
attempts to get an arm between himself and the woman.
Will you let me drive? I can't see with you ... He fires a
finger toward the windshield. Christ, what's that?

She doesn't have time to react. The impact knocks her
against the passenger side door and she feels the serrated
knife blade penetrate her flesh. She jerks the knife out
and drops it on the rubber mat floor. What the fuck? The
man spits. We hit something. What the fuck? Are you

fucking nuts, or what? Do you wanna kill us both? She scrambles for her pack, blindly searches out the car door handle, grabs, pulls, bangs her shoulder into the door and ejects herself from the still-speeding vehicle. She bounces and rolls across the shoulder and lands on the grass. The car barrels down the highway, its taillights fading to pinpricks in the distance. The woman's backpack lands several yards away from her. She stretches her arms forward, digs in with her knees and crawls toward the trees. She loses a sandal, manages to push a few extra feet. Finally, she gives up, turns over, stares up at the sky.

Crazy as a shithouse rat. She grins. Look who's calling the kettle black.

We are only as sick as our secrets.

Damn straight.

She blinks once and everything goes dark.

⌒

It's a media frenzy: Abandoned car hidden in trees along a lone stretch of highway sniffed out by dogs belonging to early morning hikers, license plate belonging to missing Toronto woman, mysterious disappearance, foul play not ruled out, packed suitcase in back of car, area known for previous instances of road-side murders, rumours of a possible serial killer at large. All the lurid elements of a sensationalistic story in the making. Victim's mother offers reward for information leading to the whereabouts. Victim's husband goes on camera to make a plea for the safe return. Victim's psychiatrist paints ominous patient profile including hostility toward herself and others as well as sexual fixations which leave her open to abusive relations. Do not discount Stockholm Syndrome. Further agrees to provide grief counselling to those closest should the situation arise. Fee negotiable.

Further rewards are offered by special interest groups as well as more local concerned citizens and businesses requesting information that may lead to the arrest and conviction. Police claim they are doing everything possible, warning that the longer it takes, the less likely are the chances of the missing woman's survival and safe return. The usual suspects are being gathered and interrogated. Bolos and APBs are being issued. DNA from hair and fabric samples is being analyzed. Promises and assurances are being made: There is no need to panic. If a heinous crime has been committed we will apprehend the sick sonofabitch responsible. ABC, NBC, CBC, CNN, CTV, FOX, CP24, CityTV and the like, delve deep into similar past cases and re-broadcast these along with recent interviews, commentary and thought-provoking analysis in order to allow the viewing audience the opportunity to share and enjoy as much information and participation as possible under the circumstances. Contact numbers have been set in place to enable anyone to easily offer information, opinions or points of view via telephone, email, Twitter, Facebook, Blogs, Livestream and so on.

Be part of the solution, not the problem.

The lines of communication are open 24/7. The boards are lit with callers.

What does the woman remember? Very little, if anything. Most of it is gone now, relegated to the part of the brain that stores useless information and empty memories. The rest is simply vague impressions: a car, a highway, an accident of some sort. Hard to say. She seems to recall a wound in her side. She feels for it with her fingers and there's nothing. Skin smooth as silk and not even the hint of a scar. None of this matters. What matters is here and now—lying on a table in a strange room, staring up at the slow revolve of a ceiling fan's dusty blades. She's naked and can feel the cool air drift across her skin; stiffen her nipples; bristle her pubic hair. She lowers her eyes and recognizes the same black crow positioned at her feet, beak open, wings spreading and folding. The woman wiggles her toes. Around one wrist is the coiled weight of the grey snake, vertical pupils fixed on her. She spots Reuben across the floor, putting a CD in the player. Like her, he's naked. He hits the play button. It's The Tragically Hip with *Killing Time*. Gord Downie sings: "I need your confidence, need to know you're mine, when it gets right down to the killing time." She wonders if everything has meaning beyond itself or if it simply *is what it is* and anything further is pure misguided human folly, wishful thinking or blind coincidence?

Chicken or egg? Background become foreground? A stone so heavy even God can't lift? Black rainbows followed by white rainbows?

Words, words, words.

Reuben walks toward her and puts out a hand. She takes it, sits up, climbs off the table onto the floor. He studies her. Her skin sparkles; it absolutely glows. Not a mark, not a blemish. He leads her to the back door, wraps a hand around the handle. He steps to one side and swings the door open. The woman is struck by a flash of blinding sunlight. She covers her face with an arm, then slowly drops it as her eyes become accustomed. She gradually takes in the scene. The sky is filled with big, fluffy white cumulus clouds sliced through by brilliant golden beams. She seems to recall a similar picture in a book she once owned as a child. Beneath the clouds grows a beautiful garden complete with cascading stream, waterfalls and a quiet pond surrounded by leafy tall trees, beautiful blooming flowers, the whole diorama alive with all manner of birds, insects and animals roaming freely and cohabiting peacefully one with the other: a deer grazes within inches of a lazing timber wolf; a raccoon play-wrestles with a coyote.

Lions among lambs, foxes among hens and so on.

The woman squeezes Reuben's hand.

Don't quit five minutes before the miracle happens.

Reuben kisses her forehead and she smiles. From somewhere close by, the desultory sound of a lone guitar emerges. Man in black intones: Hallelujah, Hallelujah!

What brave new world is this?

The two step forward. They exit the house and enter the garden, their naked bodies haloed in a blaze of brilliant white light.

THE REEVE SISTERS' TALE

In which twin sisters decide to honour
the memory of their late mother by attempting
to seduce her former lovers.

Martin enters the apartment, crosses to the kitchen where Maggie is enjoying a glass of wine.

"I received the most incredible email just as I was leaving the office." He kisses her on the cheek. "What are we drinking?"

"Pinot Grigio."

"Fantastic." He squints at the label and pours himself a glass. "Fish?"

"Teriyaki grilled salmon, wild rice with mushrooms, French green beans sautéed in garlic and sesame oil. I'm tossing a salad with prosciutto and herbed goat cheese."

"You're a marvel. Managed to stop along the way, did we? Pusateri's? I don't know how you find the time. I look at my watch and it's *ohmygod*, where did the day disappear?"

"You picked up Chinese last night. Beef and broccoli with black bean sauce. Chicken Chow Mein. Fortune cookies. Very nice."

"That was food. It was adequate. This is a feast. The wine could be, perhaps cooler." Martin adds a few cubes from the ice bucket.

"You'd do that anyway, regardless. It's what you do —ice cubes in white wine."

"I like it freezie cold, brrr. What do you say? Too low brow?"

"You can give it a shot of liquid nitrogen if it makes you happy." Maggie tops up her glass. "You mentioned a most incredible email."

"Yes. Seems a former, uh, *acquaintance* of mine died six months ago ..."

"By acquaintance, you mean ...?"

"Lover. I told you about her, I'm sure. Connie Reeve. Former student of mine. *Mature* student, yes? No hanky-panky until after the course had ended. Very much according to Hoyle."

"I seem to recall. Approached you on the final day. Said she'd had thoughts of sucking your cock while you were at the lectern. Said she was hot to fuck you. I may be paraphrasing. Words to that effect, at any rate."

"That's her." He drops another cube into his glass. "A free spirit. Hippie-dippie bohemian type. Flower child of the seventies carried into the twenty-first century. Married to a whiz IT guy so able to take the odd university course here and there, you know: Philosophy, English, Theatre ..."

"History."

"History, yes. And never for credit towards a degree, no. Always audit. Strictly on a 'knowledge for knowledge's sake' basis."

"Plus the thrill of screwing a professor or two."

"I never thought of it quite that way." Martin gives his glass a swirl and stares across the room.

"Everyone needs a hobby." Maggie's lips twist a half-smile.

"Mm."

"Was it sudden?"

"Sudden?"

"Her demise."

"Hit by a truck while riding a Vespa scooter, apparently. Died instantly."

"Tragic. Can I say, at least she had something humming between her legs when she went? Can I say that?"

"I think she'd appreciate the humour. She was that type."

"A hefty woman, you said. Plain looking. Gap-toothed. Glasses. Pointy nose. Mass of red hair. Freckles."

"I'd been recently divorced after an agonizing separation period."

"So, lonely, horny, desperate. *And* she made herself available."

"I suppose."

"Then that explains it. A winning combination. What else?"

"It lasted a few months. Then it ended ... what? Over a dozen years ago. Water under the bridge. No more to tell."

"I mean, the email." Maggie cocks her chin and raises her eyebrows.

"From her daughters. Twins. Said they're on a bit of a junket across the country in memory of their mother. Visiting her old haunts and so on. Speaking with people who knew her. A sort of metaphorical spreading of ashes. They'll be arriving in Toronto tomorrow and wonder if we can put them up for the night. Nothing fancy, they simply want to meet, talk, share some memories. What do you think?"

"Why not? So long as the memories don't get too graphic."

"Fine. I also offered dinner. They're vegetarian."

"I'll bring home Indian. Malai Kafta. Palak Paneer. Pakoras."

"Hara Chana Masala. Curried chick peas. Naan. Fantastic!"

&

The girls arrive at the door carting the usual backpacks, cotton bags plus a large folded case with a handle. The two are identical twins, right down to hairstyle and clothing choices. Two peas in a pod and bearing a strong resemblance to their mother: the build, the hair, the freckles, the wild energy. Martin guesses they must be nineteen or twenty. Everyone says hi, hey, nice to meet ya, in a wave of voices and handshakes.

"Come in, come in," Martin says. "You found the place? No problem?"

"Hi." Maggie leans in around Martin. "I'm Maggie."

"We're Chelsea," one twin says. "And Katie." They flash a look at each other. Martin and Maggie nod, like, uh-huh, OK.

"Weird, right?" The girls laugh in unison. "Don't worry

if you get it wrong. We're used to it. Even mom couldn't tell us apart. The only way is a mole. See?" One twin snaps her blouse open to reveal a dark mole above one pale breast. "If mom wanted to chew one of us out or whatever, she'd say: all right you two, show me your boobs! It was the only way." The girls find this hilarious.

"I see," Maggie says. "And what's that you're lugging?"

"Portable massage table. We're both studying massage therapy and nutrition. It's our way of saying thanks during our travels. Sort of *quid pro quo*, right? We set one of you up in the bedroom, in this case ..." The twin points a finger at Maggie.

"And you on the table down here." The other twin grins at Martin.

The couple make the usual empty noises of no need, happy to help, no bother and so on while the twins refuse to take no for an answer.

Well, OK then, it's settled. Martin shows the stairs leading to the second floor bathroom and bedrooms.

"You can go get settled and clean up before dinner. Meanwhile, can I offer you some wine?" Martin displays his glass. "We're working on a very cheeky Sauvignon Blanc from New Zealand."

"Fantastic," the twins squeal. "Are you having yours with ice?"

"Afraid so."

"No, that's great. I'll have ice too."

"Me too! I like it freezie cold. We'll just use the bathroom and be right back down." The twins clamour the stairs.

"End of the hall on the right. Bathroom next door," Maggie says. She waits for the giggles to subside and turns to Martin. "Energetic pair."

"I'll say." He goes off to pour drinks. "Not like we have to keep up, right? Looks like they're pretty capable on their own."

"They are that, no doubt."

"Nice enough though, yes? Kind of fun? Visitors. Guests."

"Yeah, fun. It'll be fun."

"And a *mass-age*." He says the word in a pseudo-pretentious manner and waggles his fingers.

"That's OK. I'm down for massage."

"Down for massage—fantastic! Like I said."

"Uh-huh. I'll heat up the oven and pop the food in bowls, you set the table."

"As you wish, madame." Martin fills two glasses with ice and wine. His body sways to some tune inside his head. He mouths a silent single word: Fantastic!

~

The twins have healthy appetites and wipe their plates clean with the naan bread. Glasses remain topped with wine. The ice bucket is replenished as needed. There's constant chatter back and forth across the table, though more so from the girls. Brazilian music plays over the stereo. It's a party atmosphere.

"Where do you head tomorrow?" Maggie asks.

"A farm outside Stratford." The twins weave their

voices in and out, beginning their own line, finishing the other's. Perfect harmony. "It used to be like a commune. Mom's wild biker period. She lived there with a greasy rocker guitar player in one of those travelling club bands. You know, the bar scene. Hundred bucks a night and all the beer you can drink. Never really went beyond that. She sang backup and played some percussion and keyboard. Other musicians used to pull up in vans and motorcycles and they'd hang out and booze and jam and smoke pot and do drugs and go crazy and whatever. Now the guy's a big name producer in the Canadian music industry. Still lives on the farm. Y'never know."

"Yeah, that's true. Tell me, how are you able to access all this information? I mean, a lot of this stuff was before you were born."

"We found mom's diaries. You know, she could come across as pretty spacey about a lot of things, but she was actually quite organized. Wrote everything down: names, places, dates, details. She saved menus and wine bottle labels and theatre programs and music concert ticket stubs and newspaper clippings and strands of hair and dried flowers and leaves and all sorts of shit. Glued or pressed or slipped between pages. Memorabilia, right? Though she went further. Kept track of people she knew years later. Whatever she came across. Which is how, you know ... Kenny the deadbeat guitar player now a freaking wheel in a suit and so on." The twins shrug and roll their eyes.

"Wow," Martin says. "Fantastic."

"Wow is right. Who'd've thunk it, eh? You wonder how she found the time."

"Internet," Maggie, who's been playing it quiet and quietly getting a warm and cozy white wine buzz on, says. "Makes it pretty easy. Maybe too easy."

"It's so true. It's like there's no such thing as privacy anymore. You teach Political Science at the university, right?"

"Yes, I do."

"There you go. Just what you were saying."

Maggie can't seem to remember what she was saying and she gives her head a slight shake. "More wine, I think, is in order. Anyone joining me?"

"We hate to spoil the party, but it is getting late and we've had a long drive and we still have to keep up our end of the bargain. Why don't you two fill your glasses, do whatever you need to do to get ready, we'll clear up the dishes ...?" Martin and Maggie raise their arms in a no-no, wouldn't think about letting you fashion and are cut off at the pass. "You have a dishwasher, yes? Easy-peasy-lemon-squeezy, as mom used to say. We'll load it up, grab a quick shower, gather our oils and meet you in fifteen. No arguments. Go!"

The couple does as told. Maggie staggers her glass and a half-full bottle of wine up to the bedroom. Martin drags a decanter of Cognac out of the cupboard and shakes it gently in front of the twins. They giggle and nod. He pours three shots, takes his into the bathroom and runs water in the sink. The twins clink glasses, throw back the contents, smack their lips, load the dishwasher and tear up the stairs.

⁓

Maggie sits on the side of the bed, wrapped in a house-coat, sipping her wine. She checks the clock as one of the twins enters.

"Fifteen minutes exactly. Excellent. Do I have the pleasure of the one with the mole or without?"

The girl wears a kimono tied with a belt of oils. She has rubber flip-flops on her feet. "Without," she says, and parts the kimono slightly with two fingers so Maggie can take a peek. "Why don't you remove the housecoat and stretch out on the bed with your arms at your side, head at the bottom." Maggie does so. "I think we can undo this as well." The girl unsnaps Maggie's bra. "In fact, it would make it a whole lot easier and a whole lot more comfortable if we get rid of it altogether. If that's OK with you?" She's already man-oeuvring the woman so as to slide the bra out from under. Maggie offers no resistance. "You have a terrific body."

"You mean, for my age."

"No, I mean you have a terrific body." The girl squirts oil into her hands and applies it to Maggie's shoulders and back. "Fit. Lean. Firm. Do you work out?"

"When you enjoy eating … and drinking … as much as I do, you have to work out. Aerobics' class three mor-nings a week, a swim at lunch, or weights, or stair climb-ing. I belong to a running club, play some tennis—badly —play some golf—worse—ride a bike. The usual."

"A healthy body and a healthy mind. Great for the sex life as well."

"Ha! After all the time and effort it takes to stay fit, who has the energy for sex?"

"That can't be true." The girl feels Maggie shrug beneath

her touch. "Uh-huh. How does this feel? Too deep? Not deep enough?"

"Feels great. You have great hands. Muscular, yet gentle. Hit all the right spots."

"Well, you know what they say, no one knows a woman's body as well as another woman."

"They say that? What? At massage school?" Maggie waits for a reply. There's nothing except the girl's fingertips exploring the flesh of her lower back.

"Anyway, you'll let me know, yes? What you need." She slips her fingers under the elastic waist of Maggie's panties. "I'm just going to lower these a smidge. Lift." She rolls the material almost to the thighs and digs her knuckles into the round flesh. Maggie lies still, low moans issuing from her mouth. The girl squirts more oil and rubs up and down Maggie's legs. "Terrific legs. Great ass." The two share a laugh at this remark.

"Thanks," Maggie says. "It's sweet of you to say."

"Do you mind?" the girl says.

"What?"

"Roll over."

~

Martin lies on his back. There's a white sheet folded between his hairy bare legs and across his crotch. His boxer shorts are hooked over a kitchen chair. His arms are at his sides and a Cognac balances on his plump belly, the glass rising and falling as he breathes. The girl leans over his face, rubbing his chest with her oiled hands.

Her kimono is loosely open at the top and Martin wonders at the prospect of a young breast tumbling free. As it is, he can't help but notice two nipples poking the thin fabric, suggesting the girl is braless.

"You have a solid chest. With very tense muscles. In fact, you're solid all over. Tough to get in deep."

"Not so solid here." Martin laughs and grabs the flab at his waist.

"You mean the love handles," the girl says, smiling.

"More like a spare tire off a semi."

"I prefer love handles." She skates her palms lower across his belly. Her breasts graze Martin's cheeks. Her thumb hits the glass and spills the Cognac. "Oops," she says, slipping quickly to one side and snatching the glass in mid-fall. She passes the glass to Martin and leans in to lap up the liquid. "Waste not, want not," she whispers. She rubs the remaining mix of saliva, Cognac and oil into his flesh. She rests her chin on his solar plexus and stares into his eyes. "Martin ..." she says.

"Yes?"

"Martin ..."

"I'm not sure I understand what's happening here."

"Martin. You've been leaving your hand where I can rub my thigh against it. You've been trying to get a good look at my tits. And you can't tell me the idea of fucking the daughter of an ex-lover doesn't excite you." She twists her head to check out his crotch. "Is that an erection I see before me?" She gently drags the sheet away and allows it to drift onto the floor.

"I didn't bring ... That is, I don't have ..."

The girl produces a condom from a pocket. She waves it at Martin and tears it open with her teeth. Martin shuts his eyes and grinds his head into the pillow.

Fantastic, he thinks.

～

Maggie's panties are down around her ankles. The girl has the flat of her hand pressed against one of Maggie's breasts and is gently rolling a nipple between her thumb and forefinger. Her other hand is situated on Maggie's pubic mound, two fingers parting the labial lips, the middle finger exciting the clitoris. When Maggie orgasms, she moans in short sharp gasps, her entire body quivers, she clenches her teeth and folds into a foetal position. The girl waits for the tremors to subside.

"I'm sorry, I suddenly have to pee. All that wine. Be right back." The girl hurries to the bedroom door.

"Go there," Maggie says, gasping. "The en suite."

"I know it sounds bizarre," the girl says. "I can never pee with someone nearby. I don't know what it is. I just sit there, needing to go, but not able."

She exits the room and reaches the top of the stairs at the same time her sister arrives. The one peels the mole from her breast and sticks it on the other. The two take a few seconds to enjoy a little shared dance action to the low volume sound of a Stan Getz Samba before they split in opposite directions.

～

"I understand where you're coming from, I think. When I visit friends or relatives or acquaintances or whatever, if I need to have a bowel movement, I'm uncomfortable, embarrassed even. It's difficult. I always carry matches with me, just in case. Which is funny, 'cause the smell of sulphur has to be, like, an even worse indicator of what's happened, right? Anyway." Martin's working on another Cognac and is pretty bombed, overall. He's naked and his shrunken penis has a damp pink glow to it. The girl kicks off her flip-flops. "You OK? We good?"

"We're pretty good," the girl says. "I was just wondering, professor ..." She holds a fresh condom in the air. "How many times does fifty-eight go into twenty?"

"Math was never my strong suit," Martin says, feeling a slight sticky twitch against his inner thigh.

"Good. Mine neither." She lets her kimono fall, skips across the hardwood and straddles Martin on the massage table. He takes a foggy look at the mole above one of her breasts. He blinks and looks again. He checks the other breast. His mouth hangs open as if to speak. The girl descends and drives her tongue between his lips, effectively silencing him.

~

"You're up early."

"Check the time. You're up late. No aerobics this morning?"

"A bit hung over for that. You made coffee." Maggie pours a cuppa. "How about you? Not hung over?"

"Totally. On my second mug and my third Tylenol."

"And the girls?"

"Gone at first light. Maybe before first light. Left with nary a trace." Martin pushes an envelope in Maggie's direction. "They did leave a note of thanks."

"Ah, youth!" Maggie ignores the envelope, pulls the lapels of her housecoat together and tightens the belt. She watches Martin tap computer keys.

"Anything interesting?"

"I'm hitting send. There!" He goes to the coffee pot. "Something interesting. I think it's interesting. An email from Connie Reeve."

"The dead ex-lover."

"Not so dead, apparently."

"Then what?"

"Don't know. She wrote and said: my daughters may drop in. STOP. They discovered my diaries. STOP. All hell broke loose. STOP. If they do drop by, have them call me ASAP. STOP. I'll explain later. FULL STOP."

"That was it?"

"That was it. FULL STOP."

"Sounds ominous. And you replied?"

"I replied. Said they were here, dinner and drinks, conversation, spent the night, et cetera, et cetera ..."

"Strange."

"Umm."

"What happened and what are they up to, do you think?"

"Don't know." Martin adds cream to his coffee. "Can you tell me something?"

"What?"

"Chelsea and Katie, right? Which was which?"

"Which was which? Good question. One had a mole above her breast. Chelsea, I think. Though it may have been Katie. Things are a bit of a haze."

"A mole, yes. Which side, left or right?"

Maggie absentmindedly checks her breasts through the housecoat. "No idea." She shakes her head. "Not a clue."

"Me neither."

"Curiouser and curiouser, said Alice." Maggie looks at Martin who rattles his mug with a spoon. "Gotta get ready for work. Dinner tonight. Thoughts?"

"Dunno. Pizza?"

"Good idea. Thin crust Quattro Stagioni. Arugula salad with grape tomatoes, oil and balsamic vinegar dressing and shaved Parmegiano-Reggiano cheese."

"Accompanied by a full-bodied Ripasso Valpolicella."

"Sounds yummy. Pizzeria Via Mercanti Neapolitan in Kensington Market, yes? Can you place the order and pick it up?"

"Can and will do." Martin turns away slightly and looks out the window.

Maggie sets her coffee cup on the table and pokes at the thank you card with her fingers. "Fantastico," she says.

Martin catches her action from the corner of an eye. He smiles, nods, sips his coffee. "Fantastico, yes. Molto Fantastico!"

A hot summer night. The large corner patio at the Dip is, as usual, a buzz of activity, with all tables crammed cheek to jowl with a mixed clientele, though mostly young people, the men dressed casually in cut-offs or shorts or jeans and T-shirts, the women in brief tight-fitting skirts or loose flowing skirts and light cotton blouses. All are shod in sandals or sneakers, cowboy boots or high heels. They eat pizza and pasta dishes and drink cold frothy beer poured from plastic pitchers or wine from litre decanters. There's a waiting list, and a similar group of people spill onto College Street. The line bends north up Clinton street. They talk, joke, text, check out their social networks, smoke and/or generally pass the time while waiting to be seated. They haven't arrived for the menu, specifically, which is of average quality and, while not unreasonably expensive, is not cheap either. No, they've gathered for the atmosphere, the history, the reputation. What reputation? The reputation of being the Dip, of course. Or moreover, the patio of the Dip. And everyone is content to stand in line for the opportunity simply to be sat and served at the Dip, despite the slow service, cramped quarters, soiled tablecloths and tolerable menu in order to say: Meet you on the patio at the Dip. Or: I was at the patio at the Dip.

Or simply: The Dip at eight and everyone understanding and knowing the place to be; to see and to be seen.

While most customers are gathered in pairs or else small to medium-sized groups, one man sits alone at a rear table with his back to the wall. He's in his mid- to late-fifties and bears a striking resemblance to the late actor Charles Laughton: roundish, fleshy with a large porcine head, thick damp lips, balding, dressed in a faded pale-blue, sweat-stained polo shirt, torn khaki shorts, worn black socks and scuffed brown loafers. He uses a paper napkin to wipe perspiration from his forehead and neck. He struggles with his breath and displays a slight wheeze. There's a wiped-clean spaghetti plate in front of him alongside an empty bread bowl. A half-litre carafe of red wine is two-thirds done while his glass is topped up. He uses a pudgy hand to bring the glass to his lips and take a sip. He smacks and licks his lips with the bulk of a fat, moist, pink tongue. He places the glass on the chequered cloth and pushes at a loose pile of papers. He takes a pen and makes a flourish at the bottom of a page, sticks the pen in his shirt pocket, leans back and drums the table with his fingertips. He straightens the loose pages and attaches a paper clip to the top left corner. Next, he pokes two fingers into his breast pocket, retrieves a playing card and tucks it under the clip. On one side of the table are strewn several other stacks of paper, also clipped, also with a playing card attached. He proceeds to put the separate stacks into one large pile and binds the lot with a black ACCO clip.

Again, he withdraws a playing card from his breast pocket and jams it underneath the metal rim.

The card is the knave of spades.

He presses his palm over the stack, picks it up and eases it into a large manila envelope. He licks the flap and seals it. He opens his shoulder bag, drops the package inside and zips the bag shut. He downs his wine, coughs and wipes his mouth with the back of a hand. The waitress approaches. Tally, skinny gal, with bare, tattooed arms, freckled face and short-cropped spiky red hair. She dumps the remains of the carafe into his empty glass.

"Another?" she asks, friendly and direct.

He takes a quick glance around, surveys the clientele and the line up. He smiles, shrugs expansively and points to the carafe.

"Another," he says. He reaches for his pen, gives it a click and hunches over a fresh sheet of paper. "Why not? The night is young, even if I'm not."

She makes with the obligatory smile, like she's heard and seen it all before, a seasoned veteran at —what?— maybe thirty-two. Maybe.

"Sure, honey," she says. "No problem." She's in a rush to keep up with the crowd.

He cocks his chin, taps the paper with the pen nib and begins to write: *While most customers are gathered in pairs or else small to medium-sized groups, one man sits alone at a rear table with his back to the wall. He's in his mid to late thirties and bears a striking resemblance to actor James Franco: slim, muscular, handsome, thin*

beard, shock of spiky black hair, piercing brown eyes.
He's dressed in an immaculate robin's egg blue silk short
sleeved shirt, white cargo shorts and Birkenstock sandals. He reaches for his cigar and taps the ash against
the glass. He takes a long slow drag and blows a thin
cloud of smoke toward the sky. The waitress approaches with a glass of red wine. The man regards the bare
tops of her ample breasts as she bends to place the glass
on the table. He smiles at her and she returns the smile.
From the woman seated near the fence, says the waitress,
with a mischievous wink. The man winks in return.

It promises to be an evening rapt in intrigue and
adventure.

ACKNOWLEDGEMENTS

Thanks to Selina Martin for the use of her song lyrics, "Johnny's Just a Boy." Also thanks to the magazines that first published some of these stories: *Scrivener Creative Review, Existere,* and *Front&Centre Magazine*. As well, to the OAC Writers' Reserve Program and the publishers who made recommendations on my behalf to help further the manuscript's completion.

ABOUT THE AUTHOR

Stan Rogal was born in Vancouver. He now lives and writes in Toronto. His work has appeared in numerous magazines and anthologies in Canada, the US and Europe, some in translation. He is the author of 21 books: five novels, five story and 11 poetry collections. He is also a produced playwright.